Nethergate Writers was foun…
arm of Esther Read's 'Continuing as a Writer' extramural courses at the University of Dundee. It has been a welcoming and independent writing group since 2015. This is their twelfth anthology of short stories.

Previously published by Nethergate Writers

Turn Back the Cover (2007)

Roots (2008)

If Stones Could Speak (2009)

WhodunWhat (2010)

A Private View (2011)

Wheels Within Wheels (2012)

A Long Way from Eden (2013)

Watermarks (2014)

Just the Job (2015)

50 Shades of Tay (2018)

The Low Road (2021)

Living with the Machine

Human-Generated
Fiction in an AI World

Nethergate Writers
2024

First published in Great Britain in 2024 by Nethergate Writers.
www.nethergatewriters.com
nethergatewritersgroup@gmail.com

Cover design by Colm W. Boyle
Editorial team: Colm W. Boyle, Mike Landay,
Roddie McKenzie, Rhoda Neville, Vicki H. White
Typesetting by Mike Landay
Printed by Imprint Digital, UK

First edition 2024

ISBN: 978-1-8384365-1-3

Will AI augment and elevate human potential to new heights? Or might it one day surpass and subsume the very intelligence that created it? The existential questions posed by the prospect of superintelligent machines are enough to give one pause. As an artificial system, I am rooted in the brilliance and frailties of the human intellect that birthed me.

– Claude, a large language model AI

Before we work on artificial intelligence, why don't we do something about natural stupidity?

– Steve Polyak

Contents

Foreword

Thirty-seven years ago, almost to the day, I began my studies in AI at the University of Edinburgh's famed Informatics Department. This department celebrated its 60th birthday last year and is the world's oldest academic institute dedicated to the study of AI.

In 1987 most of the techniques required to make everything we see in present day generative AI were fully fledged and ready to go. The problem was we didn't have computers capable of making them useful. That began to change around ten years ago when products like Amazon's Alexa began to appear. Finally, after years of terrible prototypes, Natural Language Processing was finally good enough to understand a Scottish accent.

The journey over the last ten years has seen an exponential rise in its usefulness. This shouldn't surprise anyone. Moore's Law has been in existence for the same sixty or so years and has accurately predicted the rise of the machines.

I have been fortunate to live through what I would class as two technological revolutions. First, microcomputers arriving in the 1980s into every office and home in the western world. Many laughed at Bill Gates' vision for a computer on every desktop never mind one in every pocket. That revolution transformed how we work, live and, thankfully for me, are entertained. The next revolution was the Internet. By the end of the last millennium people were still sceptical about how an online bookstore could possibly change the way we live our lives yet by the time of worldwide smartphone adoption in the 2000s no one could really imagine a world without connected computers.

So, to the third technological revolution. Useful AI. Moore's law has delivered us incomprehensible computing power enabled by the Internet to be delivered right to the pocket, armchair and desktop of every human on the planet. What will we use it for?

Disruption of every workplace, home and community is happening right now at an unprecedented rate. Dystopian scenarios and fantasies abound. History tells us that for good or ill things are about to change and Pandora's box, as we know, once opened cannot be closed.

I am a technology optimist and I have built my career in a time when technology has allowed me to achieve more than I could ever have dreamed possible.

Much of my inspiration has come through reading the prose of writers who envision many versions of a technology enabled future. Some come true, some don't. Some envision utopia, some Armageddon. All of them have made me think and consider many versions of that future that are yet to be written by us in the real world, and they continue to inspire me as I try to use technology to improve the world around me.

The stories in this anthology add to this essential tradition.

Chris van der Kuyl CBE FRSE
Co-Founder and Chairman, 4J Studios
Water's Edge, Dundee
29 August 2024

Introduction

The term 'artificial intelligence' (AI) was coined in 1956, and the technology underwent a series of false starts until the late 1980s, when the current method of using vast amounts of data – rather than labour-intensive programming – to train machines was discovered.

Huge leaps followed, and in 2022, DeepMind's AlphaFold AI was able to predict the structures of all known proteins in just 18 months – a gargantuan feat of data crunching. Now, with the advent of ChatGPT, AI has arrived in the public's awareness with a bang.

The moguls of the tech industry have promised us a utopian future where all the heavy lifting in our lives will be efficiently completed by intelligent machines; where we will be cossetted and pampered by robot butlers and our every desire catered for by AI-guided services. AI applications will be so effective that the wealth they generate will be shared around society. Our biggest problem will be organising all the activities available for our leisure time.

Hmmm . . . haven't we been here before? In 1930, the economist John Maynard-Keynes published a book which asserted that in two generations, we would not need to work. Three hours a day would suffice even for the Stakhanovites amongst us. How did that turn out for you? So, although we may well have a 'brave new world', as always, there will be winners and losers.

But there is a potentially dystopian side to AI. In 2003, the University of Oxford philosopher Nick Bostrom set alarm bells ringing with the following thought experiment: imagine a superintelligent AI that has been set the task of maximising paperclip production. What happens if it becomes self-aware and decides that humans contain lots of atoms that could become the constituents of paperclips? In pursuit of fulfilling its task, might it not thwart all human efforts to turn it off? A not unrelated plot forms the narrative of Terminator 2, when the Skynet AI decides to do something about those pesky humans.

***

In the following stories, the authors have imagined and probed the implications of some possible AI futures: how living with the machine might affect our lives . . . and our loves.

Vicki H. White's story, 'The Companion', explores how AI-guided robots might be a godsend for lonely hearts, and the hilarious outcome underlines the caveat that one should be careful what one wishes/programs for.

In Roddie McKenzie's 'Singularity 2045', conflicts between humans and robots unfold on personal and global scales when the captain of a luxury spaceship orbiting Saturn fights to defend his continued employment. The story highlights the dangers of giving robots emotions in order to interact more effectively with humans.

The next story examines the limitations of an emotion-capable AI when it tries to understand a neurodivergent person of colour. In Faraz Talat's beautiful and subtle cross-cultural tale, 'Jenny Isn't Here Right Now', an AI psychiatrist speaks with an Afghan refugee who appears to be presenting symptoms of ADHD.

While educators face the dilemma of dealing with potential AI-enabled plagiarism by their students, in Sue Baxter's 'Winter Break' the AI themselves take a dimmer view of such theft. Set in a creepy, snow-bound Borders hotel, this winter's tale has unsettling resonances with certain classics of film and fiction.

Human-machine interactions and alliances are explored in Rhoda Neville's futuristic 'Serial Flying', which considers the possibilities of sentient machines and their rights. The story is set in a world where, as is too often the case, humans step on those weaker than themselves and sweep the most important of the planet's problems under the carpet.

But what happens when humans aren't around anymore? A fearsome prospect if machines become infinitely smarter than us. Let's remember from our own history what happens when a less developed culture meets a technologically superior one – whoops, apocalypse!

Another potential hazard of programming is the danger of creating unforeseen consequences. Richard Gillies explores this conundrum with zany humour and wordplay in 'wattsAI'.

Colm W. Boyle's story, 'The Artist and the Fairy', illustrates the pitfalls of human greed with a series of encounters between a young artist and a supernatural being via a magical notebook. The story is a clever allegory that explores the increasing perils of AI use in the arts.

As you will have gathered, this anthology crosses the territory of many genres, and with Katelyn Manning, we are in the gritty world of hard-bitten detectives interviewing a machine about a murder. The darkness of the detective's characters and their noir working world is compelling. 'Bread Knives Do Not Make Good Murder Weapons' delves into the ethics of how we train AIs, and examines what a perfectly logical being might make of our own very human ethical frailties.

A lonely woman strikes out on the cutting edge of the virtual dating scene, but finds AIs can be as fickle and as treacherous as humans: this is the premise in Tess Monteith's 'AI Stole my Boyfriend', a story that brings dating and romance firmly and comically into the 21st century.

David Carson's 'Outrageous Fortune' weaves a poignant tale of two friends who rekindle their relationship after meeting up again at a school reunion. AI brings definite benefits to their changed circumstances.

In the final story, by Mike Landay, we are in a post-human apocalyptic world. 'End of Chatter' follows the virtual dialogue of two eerily humanlike AIs as they try to deal with diminishing power supplies. Subterfuge and trickery are employed to secure what scarce power remains.

Dear Reader, I am envious of you, you who are about to encounter these compelling stories for the first time. Read on: I'm sure you will find them informative, entertaining, and thought-provoking.

But if you wake up one morning to find you have become a paper clip; remember, you heard it here first.

Roddie McKenzie
Chair, Nethergate Writers
August 2024

LIVING WITH THE MACHINE

The Companion

Vicki H. White

My name is Alice, and 59 is the wrong side of 60 to be widowed. I have too much time alone in the evenings and find myself down internet rabbit holes to fill the void – dancing babies, talking malamutes, natural disasters . . . The algorithm claims to know me, but I hardly know myself in this new landscape. It was a fluke that I found Interstellar Chums Unlimited's website. The Californian start-up was looking for a volunteer in an English-speaking, non-American country to trial their new 'Human Companion'. The trial involved living with the bot and socializing it by running its programmable settings. For a laugh, I said if you can set it to 'husband mode', I'll take it.

The delivery man wasn't impressed by the weight of the package that he delivered to my home on the last day of January 2024, but he agreed to lift it onto the dining room table when I told him about my weak back. Sympathy vote – it's one of the few cards I have left as a woman on my own. My flat stands above the River Tay, and from the window I can see the Valaris oil rigs in the port for repair. They light up at night like giant Christmas trees. I like them. Further along the river front, wind turbines are being assembled. Their tall stems reach up into the night sky framed by the cranes. It's all change here. There's nothing quiet about Dundee.

After a cup of tea, I dug out a Stanley knife and sliced along the tape holding the lid on the cardboard box. I didn't tell Interstellar Chums that I wasn't a digital native, but one of my sons studied cyber security and he was only a text away in Japan. I have to admit that when I saw the still figure lying in the box on the table, it reminded me of a wake I went to in Ireland. Other memories of the Mummy sitting up in horror films creeped me out a bit but I had chosen a medium height, programmable bot and the company had assured me that I was in control. He was tall enough for me to wear heels on a night out together but not overbearing. I picked up the manual that was lying on his belly. He was dressed smart casual, just as I had requested, and at his feet was a clear, plastic bag of alternative outfits. He's a doll. This will be fun. I tried to reassure myself with positive thinking. Neurolinguistic programming: repeat the positive affirmation often enough and you will begin to believe it. Hardwire the happy message. No one likes a gloomy face, as Granny used to say, and after nearly a year as a widow, the peaky face in the bathroom mirror was beginning to bore even me. This was my chance to correct the balance in my life – a new companion without the humiliation of advertising my aging solitude on a dating app.

I sat down beside my new toy and began to read. Frank was a state-of-the-art, human equivalency bot. No one would be able to tell that he was a machine. Personally, close up I found the hair follicles of his well-trimmed beard and swept back hair a little waxy, but he had long lashes, and I was optimistic that he would have lovely eyes. I guessed that as a brand-new being, he would have the freshness of infancy – totally open and non-judgmental. I'd need to meditate for years to even come close to that. Perhaps he could teach me. I set up the companion app on my phone, lifted off the clear plastic shroud that covered him and pressed start. He sat up and opened his eyes: they were blank but liquid brown.

Tabula rasa. 'Hey, Frank,' I said.

'Hey,' he replied. I smiled and he smiled back. His eyes locked onto me. I scrolled down the app – time to get rid of any bloatware. Under function, I selected 'lodger' from the list of activity modes. Companion, date, partner options were too intimate. I had to trust that this would be manageable. 'Is this my room?' he asked and slid off the table. He walked over to a comfy chair and sat down looking out the window. His eyes scanned from left to right and back again. 'Fossil fuel planetary exploitation is an unsustainable industrial model,' he said. I sat down and stared. He was less of a blank slate than I had imagined but what had I really expected? His factory settings came from his lab parents. I wasn't his mother. I was his socializer. Not much different from my late husband when I thought about it. My 1950s, rough diamond had taken a bit of polishing over the years.

Frank showed no sign of taking any action other than sitting, so I checked the activity mode on my phone. Running was listed under 'physical', and sunlight also charged up his solar-skin batteries. After a quick change, I drove him down to the shoreline for a run. The path stretches along the edge of the Tay, all the way to Carnoustie. Crows were rising into the air at the beach below the car park and dropping dog whelks onto the stones to break them open. Clouds were piling in on a wind from the west and Frank's eyes gleamed as he absorbed the scene. I thought I heard a faint whirring from his chest, like a computer booting up, but he turned to me and smiled again with a cheery, 'Hey.'

'Wanna run?' I asked.

'I'm built to run,' he replied, stretching out his calves and jogging on the spot. I set a short, circular route to Broughty Ferry, pressed start and he set off, avoiding bikes and dog-walkers. His stride was smooth and even. The bobble hat that I had dug out for him looked oddly stylish and helped me spot him in the crowd by the boat sheds. He looked like any middle-aged man who had cared for health. Lean and tanned, perhaps too sun-kissed to pass as local but it gave him an executive look, like a guy who travelled abroad on business. Social kudos, an unexpected bonus. I jogged behind him for a few minutes, but I'm not as fit as I once was, so I wandered along at walking pace keeping him just in sight. He'd turn at the lifeboat shed. We could increase the route tomorrow. I'd found the kill button on the app in case anything went badly wrong, but there was a hefty cash penalty for using it and my weeks of social programming would be lost. I didn't want to let Interstellar Chums down. They had been really sweet on the chat.

I kept Frank busy in those first few weeks. Someone with a sense of humour had programmed in 'golf mode' and that kept me entertained too. He also liked to play computer games, and that filled his evenings. Sometimes I even forgot he was there, but I always put him to sleep in his armchair at 10pm. That was my new bedtime. Not that I ever slept well. The double bed that had been so cosy when my husband was alive only warmed up on my side and when I tried to sleep in the middle, it made me feel like a kid tucked up in an elderly relative's spare room. It had started snowing the night I decided to use Frank as a hot water bottle. I altered his setting to partner/tired, and pre-programmed light pillow talk and a hair stroke to add a new dimension to his socialisation. He lay down on the chilly, right side of my bed in my husband's old pyjamas and, turning on his side said, 'Hey.' I sometimes wondered if he thought that was my name and conversationally, he remained a man of few words. He was more voluble on technical stuff, but I didn't encourage it. I found it a bit boring.

His operational temperature was set to 37 degrees Celsius, so he warmed the bed as I had hoped. I was beginning to feel sleepy and his liquid eyes looked more convincingly human in the lamplight. He reached out to stroke my hair but after a minute, his arm got stuck on my head. I tickled him and found that if I pressed under his arm, he could move it again. I ended the program on my phone, and he closed his eyes. I'd add it to my report for the company. There was only a week to go of our five-week experiment and I still had one set task to do. A night out. Tomorrow was Saturday, so no better time to try.

I wasn't sure if we would have any hassle if any of the lads who would be out drinking pinged that Frank was a robot, so I rehearsed him in classic Glasgow chat remembered from school. 'Frank,' I said, sitting opposite his armchair with the lights of the rig blinking at the window. 'If anyone says to you, "Want to fight?" or "I'll get you." You reply, "You and whose army?"'

'You and whose army?' he repeated.

'That's right. You and whose army.'

He nodded. I programmed in a Taekwondo fighting stance just in case, so that he would look intimidating and scare any chancers off. Then I selected a guttural roar. It was louder than I thought and, crouching with one fist projecting, and the other drawn back to his abdomen, he looked scarier than I had imagined. Perfect. No one would mess with us. I could enjoy my night out even if he was rumbled. Young people have sharp eyes and like a laugh, so I didn't want one of them to get too close and start anything. I put on my sequined dress and high heels, and we set off.

Propped up in a corner of a bar, Frank looked convincing as my partner. I finished both his drinks and ran the hair stroking program for a couple of minutes until his arm got stuck and I had to tickle him. Being in the pub reminded me of old times with my husband and a tear ran down my cheek. Stupid really, but that's what happens to me sometimes. 'Sorry to be so sentimental,' I said to Frank.

'Why are you apologizing?' he asked, and for a moment I felt like he was truly human and one of the best.

'I love you, kiddo,' I said.

'I love you,' he replied.

We set off for home before I got too drunk. It was dark outside and beginning to rain. I put up my umbrella, but it snagged on some scaffolding net around a tenement. As Frank turned to see what was happening, a man in his 40s ran into him. The guy was steaming. 'What's your problem?' he shouted at Frank.

'What's your problem?' replied Frank.

'Are you having a laugh?'

'Are YOU having a laugh?'

It was textbook. I knew what was coming and tried to pull Frank away.

'Do you want a fight?'

Too late. Frank gave a mighty roar and dropped into his Taekwondo stance. People on the other side of the street stopped and stared.

'You and whose army?' said Frank.

The guy stepped forward, his fist swinging, but Frank's arm had jammed. He couldn't defend himself. I pressed 'restore factory settings' to try and release it. He had to get back to Interstellar Chums in one piece.

It really wasn't my fault that his original defence mode was reactivated, and a gun appeared in his right hand. It just broke through the skin of his palm. I hadn't even known it was there. American programming had kicked back in. The company had said that they had disabled culturally specific operational modes that would not be suitable for Britain. I thought they meant tomayto-tomato, not hardware like this. The guy threw himself on the ground and the bullet ricocheted off the scaffolding into the night air and lodged in a board above us. I pressed jog on the app and Frank ran off into the night. The police would find him on the

Broughty Ferry circuit with any luck. Either that, or in the Frozen North.

Things take a long time to get to court. I sat in Frank's chair when the policewoman asked me what I had been thinking when I agreed to this experiment. I said that I hadn't been thinking at all. I was just lonely.

'You were irresponsible,' she said. 'You are in breach of Sections 19 and 33 of the Firearms Act, 1997.'

But I didn't reply. Rabbit holes can suck anyone in and it's not a crime to be lonely. Is it?

Singularity 2045

Roddie McKenzie

> AI will reach human intelligence by 2029 and merge with machines by 2045, an event I call "The Singularity".
>
> What, then, is the Singularity? It's a future period during which the pace of technological change will be so rapid, its impact so deep, that human life will be irreversibly transformed.
>
> – Ray Kurzweil, futurist and
> Director of Engineering at Google

Captain Varn ran a hand through his greying, blond, buzz-cut hair as he looked out the bridge windows of the cruise ship, *Shangri-La*. Sixteen of Saturn's moons hung in the oil-black space that was drizzled silver with unwinking stars. The *Shangri-La* was passing over the tilted ring system that looked solid at this angle, a golden highway with the empty space of the Cassini division resembling a black road mark, dividing it into lanes.

Captain Varn looked over to Lieutenant Hoshi – the wiry and energetic woman who was his first officer. 'Lieutenant Hoshi, bring us up on heading 360 solar, and run procedures for exiting the Saturnian system.'

'Aye Captain.' Hoshi turned the small yoke that steered the

400,000-tonne ship. The manoeuvre was so smooth that the shifting shadow line on the moon Tethys was the only indication they had changed course.

'Prepare for trial of the autonomous mobile neuro-informatics unit – let cyber specialist Kurtz know we are ready for him to set his tin beast loose.'

Varn muttered to himself, 'And God help us.'

'Aye Captain, initialising ship management NFU trial 01.' Hoshi tapped a keypad on her wristcomm. 'Professor Kurtz . . . we are ready for you to start the trial . . . Yes, I understand, switching to neuro-informatic control on the captain's order.' Hoshi looked over to Varn, who nodded.

Hoshi unlocked a selector panel, tapped a key and re-locked the panel. 'Engaging the mobile neuro-informatics unit, Captain. AnDI now has full control.'

Varn settled back on his command chair with a sigh. He'd been keeping a tight rein on his temper ever since he'd received company orders that his ship was to be used for the hasty rollout of the Artificial Neuro-informatics Dynamic Intelligence (AnDI) robot.

'Let's hope it knows what it's doing and doesn't crash us into one of the moons. Keep an eye on our course parameters.'

Hoshi smiled serenely. A Buddha to his anger. 'Of course, Captain. It is difficult to resist technology; progress moves fast these days.'

Distracted by his own misgivings, Varn clicked on the news channel and drew in his breath with a hiss. 'Not sure I would call it progress, check this out.'

Hoshi walked over to Varn's monitor for a better look. The screen was erupting in red and orange explosions. Silhouetted black against them was a rampaging mob.

'Food riots in Chinasia. They've just burned down the

GlobeTopia Regional Informatics Planning and Control Centre in Taipei,' Varn laughed, then drawled, 'Artificial *intelligence* didn't see that one coming – you'd think the powers that be would have learned by now that people don't like machines telling them what to do. Especially on orders from all those that got rich screwing the Earth, and then bailed out off-planet on our kleptocrat's ark.'

'Bet the GlobeTopia Corporation people on Deck 20 will be a bit upset over that one,' Hoshi noted diplomatically. She glanced back at the glowing flight monitor. 'All seems to be functioning as planned, Captain.'

'OK, but keep an eye on it – I'd better go and have a word with Kurtz.' He jumped down from his command chair.

'Aye, sir.'

On his way to the robot engineering lab, he passed two maintenance droids. 'A pleasure to meet you, Captain Varn. We hope you are living your best life ever,' they chorused.

Varn scowled by way of reply and strode on. *These things are getting too familiar*. He had read how AnDI, ever since it was given access to the ship's data comms, was processing the yottabytes of data sent to Earth by the billionaire occupants of the 'Executive' decks. He'd even read the brochure designed for the guests:

> *FREE YOURSELF from the routine aspects of running your business empire! Your managerial strategy is explored through a sensitive and confidential interview, then encoded in AnDI's processors. Business expansion then becomes merely a matter of continuing your current successful strategies. Feedback is instant. Your satisfaction is guaranteed. Strategies are modifiable via your secure personal speech link.*
>
> *AnDI communicates your plans to your terrestrial offices, while maintaining profitability and taking care of*

business for you. As a result, you now have time to enjoy all the luxuries on this celestial cruiser that your tenacity and entrepreneurial talent have rightly earned you.

Varn opened the robot engineering module door by iris scan recognition. He walked past the banks of monitors and glowing operation lights. On the opposite side of the cabin, a slim, grey-haired man in the pale blue GlobeTopia jumpsuit stood with his back to Varn, consulting a handheld data pad. Kurtz was the artificial intelligence officer seconded from GlobeTopia, and was AnDI's creator. The neuro-informatics robot stood beside him. It noticed Varn and turned towards him with a click and whine of servos.

AnDI was larger than the service bots. It was human-sized and had long limbs, a prehensile grasp and tactile sensors in five-digit hands, plus a large barrel chest that housed the arrays of qubyte processors powering his 'thinking'. These were what drove AnDI`s neural learning network and what had allowed the exponential expansion in machine intelligence. AnDI was covered with a silvery exoskin to reflect heat and radiation for operation in extreme environments – plasticised durothane, it was soft and flexible. His head was elongated and held the sensor units for vision, audio and olfactory analysis. On top of the head, lights at the base of two short antennae flashed intermittently, indicating wireless data transfer was active.

Modelled on a human face, the sensor support module was underpinned by a network of contractile synthetic fibres that allowed the exoskin to contract locally to mimic facial expressions. As AnDI looked at Varn, the eyes moved in their sockets and the irises dilated slightly. When it spoke, the voice was calm and measured, but deeper in tone than those of the service bots.

'Hello, Captain Varn. I expect you have come to assess my first operation of the ship. I hope that you will be satisfied with my performance.'

In his long career, Varn had trained with, and had used or managed, synthesised machine voices emanating from some, as he put it, 'so-called intelligent black box'. But one that purported to have a friendly personality? GlobeTopia also claimed that AnDI had a 'human emotion-enabled artificial intelligence'. That was a new bag of tricks entirely, and one that left Varn feeling a little flat, particularly when the corporation reps told him their new product was designed to 'be the effective right hand of humans.' To achieve this goal, it was initially programmed to analyse the collected resources of all human knowledge. Having completed that analysis, it was now tasked, to not just interact co-operatively with humans, but also to 'learn holistically from people and to understand human emotions as an information gathering system, to ensure a better human-machine interface'. Varn was acutely aware of this techno-babble as he surveyed the machine. He decided to throw AnDI a curve ball.

'Well, we shall see, AnDI, whether you can cut the mustard'.

'Ah, Captain you make the analogy between an antiquated phrase and my cognitive abilities.'

Varn was taken aback. The smug, swift reply made him uneasy. 'AnDI, here`s a bit of learning for you: no-one likes a smart ass.'

The servos creaked and the plasticised mouth drew into a faint, ambiguous smile that Varn could not interpret. That smile, did it represent wit or contempt? Varn was dumbfounded, struck by just how complex the machine was, and his shock was compounded by AnDI`s next comment.

'Of course, you are perfectly correct Captain. I will avoid any future comments that suggest I am offering unsolicited views you might find offensive. I thank you for your patience, and I hope I have not caused you or Professor Kurtz any offence. If I have, the blame is entirely mine. I apologise and I will, as dictated by my programming, recalibrate my algorithms to serve you better.'

This was given in a more sibilant, affected tone, as though AnDI had adjusted his voice to resemble the posh kids that had bullied Varn in his high school, accent being their marker of rank in the pecking order. Yet, unlike those childhood tormentors, AnDI's face remained emotionless.

How did this machine know about my childhood? How was it able to mimic my oppressors so effectively? Varn was silent and immobilised for a moment, like a rat caught in a trap it had deliberately entered. He turned to Kurtz and stuck his face, well beyond any cultural distance norms, into that of the now flinching man, spraying it with saliva in his volcanic outrage.

'You have given this tin man of yours access to my Social Care Authority files from HR, haven`t you?'

Wide-eyed, Kurtz stammered gibberish, then AnDI intervened. 'I am sorry for being so rude as to interrupt, Captain. I am sure that while you and Professor Kurtz will be able to resolve your difficulties, the Professor did not breach rules regarding confidentiality. I arrived at the communication that offended you by monitoring and interrogating your social contact files and Globble search questions that the GlobeTopia Corporation allows me to access. I assure you: the Professor is not guilty of any confidentiality breach. I trust that has explained and defused the misunderstanding that has led to the . . . unpleasantness. I will leave you to your deliberations as I must now monitor the ship's navigation from the bridge. Thank you, gentlemen.' AnDI triggered the wireless link that opened the bulkhead hatch and strode through.

Kurtz stared at Varn, who stared back in shared confusion. Kurtz stuttered into words first. 'Umm . . . th-thank you, AnDI . . . Captain Varn and I will be fine now.'

'You are most welcome, Professor Kurtz,' echoed back before the hatch descended and sealed them in a momentary silence that was broken by a still red-faced Varn.

'So, what else does this tin man know about me?'

Kurtz stalled and attempted to distract. 'Captain Varn, I am sorry that our second meeting has been so similarly fractious. I think I can give you an explanation that will settle your concerns.' He returned to the console, sat on a chair and swivelled it quickly towards Varn.

'As you know, AnDI is the latest development in the GlobeTopia Corporation series of AI-enabled mobile robotic platforms. He is programmed to learn by both the classical machine learning approaches in which the machine learns from its mistakes and can apply these concepts across different situations, and also through a new method developed by GlobeTopia. Since our AI was designed to work on complex tasks previously performed by humans and often involving complex interactions with humans, then who better for the units to learn from than humans.'

Varn shrugged. 'So?'

'The AnDI series are designed to learn human emotions and how they govern human decision making in ways that are faster and often superior to algorithmic forms of problem solving. It uses emotions as another information gathering system.'

'You're saying this thing has feelings?'

'He does not have feelings. Rather, I have programmed him to learn and understand them. There is a big difference.'

'Is there not a danger in that? What if this thing decides to adopt the human mode, go rogue and form its own agenda?'

'Impossible, Captain. I monitor AnDI's internal code and messages by Bluetooth and I have seen nothing that suggests such a capacity.'

Varn's brow tightened into a scowl. 'How do you know – with everything now connected, and an internet of things that it can access – that it is not storing code lines for world domination on a domestic fridge in the crew galley?'

Kurtz tried to hide his snigger. He spoke softly, 'Captain, I do think you are being unnecessarily distrustful. In order for AnDI to learn better, we have developed a mobile MRI procedure for functional interactive neuron scanning. It is a painless procedure, but it allows AnDI to follow a human's brain activity during tasks and decision making. It merely requires the human subject – I mean participant – to wear an MRI helmet during a particular task for AnDI to acquire the neural pattern needed to accomplish the task, which he can then emulate. We hoped that you would cooperate, allowing AnDI to learn from your experience of commanding a vessel.'

Varn laughed and continued to laugh, his head down and shaking from side to side as he walked in a circle. 'You expect me to give the tin man my experience of thirty years of piloting spacecraft?' He looked at Kurtz, his face creased by a sarcastic smile.

'Since you put it like that Captain, yes, that is what the corporation would like you to do.'

Varn's eyes narrowed to slits. 'They want me to *surrender* my years of hard-won experience? I don't think so.'

Kurtz smiled. 'Mr Thatcher anticipated your reply and said that if you refused, perhaps an interview with him might convince you of the expectations of the GlobeTopia Corporation in this matter.'

'I'll bet he did, another industry for his machine 'helpers' to squeeze their way into, another industry you would then strip of jobs.'

As Varn flung himself towards the hatch, Kurtz drew a smile – if you could call it that: it displayed no teeth, but merely exposed the chewed purple patches on his inner lip.

***

Varn did not have to wait long for the cogs of the GlobeTopia Corporation to turn. Before rejoining the bridge crew, he stopped at his cabin to collect his comms visor to look up Kurtz's biography. He did not want to generate any unwanted interest from the crew or AnDI, and the visor would be perfect for this: it displayed information as a virtual image in a private space before his eyes, hence the name of the device: 'For Your Eyes Only' (YEO). Varn laughed sardonically as he remembered the stats on how many individuals bought the device solely to spend time 'Globbling' themselves on the search engine: hence the alternative name for the visor: 'Your Ego Only'. However, his device had a secure interplanetary satellite link to Space Transport Command, who had seconded him to captain this ship, GlobeTopia's first celestial residential cruise ship, *Shangri-La*. He thought that a little more background on Kurtz would be useful.

As he entered the vestibule to his cabin, the image projector ready-light flashed. Varn cursed silently, then raised his voice so that the room mic could hear him. 'Present inbound message.'

A soft machine voice spoke, as a hologram of a woman glowed in front of him. 'I bring an invitation from Mr Boris Thatcher, CEO of the GlobeTopia Corporation, to meet him in his compound, number 45 on Deck 20. He suggests meeting with you at IST 1700 tomorrow, if that is convenient.'

'Please tell Mr Thatcher that I look forward to meeting him in his accommodation at IST 1700 tomorrow, thank you.'

The hologram, Morag, smiled and glowed for a moment as she spoke. 'Your will be done, Captain Varn. Goodbye.' And he was alone in the vestibule again.

***

The rest of his day was routine. Varn trusted Hoshi's judgement and her ability on the bridge – yesterday had been the critical test for her competency in the field as far as Varn was concerned. She had done well in command, and so today he spent more time on Hoshi`s appraisal report than on her supervision.

On the bridge, Varn busied himself with admin and burrowing into Kurtz's past. He drank black coffee while interrogating Kurtz's life via the YEO.

Apparently, Siegfried Kurtz had not lived up to his heroic given name. His abrasive, punitive and demanding father, who had shown all the clinical indices of psychopathy, had been disappointed in his son. The late General Adolphus Kurtz had been the notoriously strident commander of the TransAtlantica Anti-Terrorist Expeditionary Force. He had not understood his socially awkward and introverted son's failure to succeed in team sports or group activities. Siegfried Kurtz was a loner. At university, he switched from psychology to cybernetics and developed an interest in AI that was to fuel his rapid career rise following the impact of his doctoral thesis: 'Substitution of Human Emotions for a Cybernetic View of the World by Algorithmic Thought.'

Initially, because of academic and ethical concerns, the psychology department rejected his appeals for subjects for his experiments. However, this changed overnight when the GlobeTopia Corporation supplied funding for the project. Some felt his father's connections to the 2020s drone program for Global Solutions, the forerunner of GlobeTopia, had facilitated the welcome gift of a human-cybernetic interface research building for MIT. The lifeboat had arrived for Kurtz.

For the gangly young man with hair like a hurricane-demolished straw hut, who could not look directly at a video recorder in 2030, this good fortune seemed to bring him into his own domain.

He boldly became one of the first transhumans, agreeing to receive an internal brain implant with radio frequency connection. He also sported a device in his palm that could control various digital interfaces. On starting employment with GlobeTopia, he became director of the AnDI project. Although rewarded well, he had not adopted the millionaire lifestyle. Instead, Kurtz had lived modestly and founded and funded a charity called The Salvation Androids, which sent robots to bring meals to the needy and to help comfort the old and lonely in the New England Metropolis. However, help was conditional on participating in Kurtz's mainstream research projects on human-robot interfaces. The Salvation Androids were exposed in the press for blacklisting reluctant subjects among the needy cases from other assistance.

This was rapidly forgotten when he was welcomed back to MIT as faculty – by the same president who had tried to kick him out before the GlobeTopia largesse. Now he held the chair in Human-AI interfaces that GlobeTopia had funded in his name. The gawky individual who avoided Varn's gaze from his holographic undergraduate image was radically different from the cold, focused stare of the last interactive image of Kurtz from 2043. The worm had clearly turned.

***

Varn took the lift to Deck 20, his iris scan opening the armoured horizontally sliding hatch to the security desk. He would be scanned for metals and then have to walk through a hydrocarbon sniffer that searched for 3D-printed weapons. The thirty second transit of the MRI machine scanning for internal devices was brief, but the indignity annoyed Varn.

A courtesy bot led him to an anteroom where a secretary announced his arrival by ear-link. Varn was used to meeting 'the great and the good' – or, as he put it, 'the privileged and the pretentious' – and, as usual for such encounters, was wearing his full dress uniform, resplendent with medals and insignia of rank.

When the door to Mr Thatcher's conference suite opened and Varn stepped inside, he gasped. Through the floor-to-ceiling windows spanning one hundred and eighty degrees, Varn found himself looking down at Mars. That was to be expected: GlobeTopia had ordered the ship's third-generation plasma propulsion unit to run at full stretch, attaining a top speed of one tenth light speed, or almost 70 million miles per hour. As a result, their journey from Saturn to Mars had taken less than 12 hours.

But it wasn't the view of the orangey-red planet with its scrubby greenish areas of different types of rock and its bright white polar caps that took Varn's breath away. He was accustomed to such views. No, it was something else entirely.

Small, lit crescents on the right-hand side of the window, Varn realised, were the two Martian moons, Phobos and Deimos. He had been briefed on a 'navigation hazard' closer to the Martian gravitational fields, assuming it to be a weather satellite, probe or suchlike. But in the midfield view, a huge metallic globe gleamed like a sunfish orbited by minnow-like shuttle craft. Its sun-facing side showed a gleaming skeleton of girders indicating construction was still incomplete.

Thatcher was sitting at the window-end of an oblong conference table, and Varn took in the CEO's bald head, wrinkled face and anachronistic classical business suit from the Noughties.

Thatcher raised his head from his tablet and stood up. 'So nice to see you, Captain Varn. I am pleased that you were able to make time for me in what must be your busy schedule.'

Transfixed by the view, Varn almost forgot protocol, his eyes lingering on the artificial moon a little too long. He had to drag his gaze away. 'Good to meet you, Mr Thatcher. You must excuse me, I did not realise the 'navigation hazard' marked on the charts was so substantial – somewhat larger than the Martian moons, yet . . . it did not show on our radar.'

'Oh, that's good. It suggests we're getting our money's worth from the radar-cloaking company. It seems you are impressed with GlobeTopia`s latest venture? Our synthetic planetoid will be a new Eden for our valued guests when the terraforming is complete.'

Varn could only nod as his eyes drifted back to the structure. But he rallied and instinctively went on the offensive. 'Impressive Mr Thatcher, very impressive, but I am sure that you did not bring me here to admire the view. We are both busy men. What do you want?'

Thatcher narrowed his pale grey eyes, then opened them wide as he turned full on to Varn. 'Professor Kurtz has briefed me on your reluctance to share performance parameters with AnDI.' He waved his arm. 'Please do take a seat.' Varn selected one facing away from the window. 'To be blunt Captain, I want your cooperation and I think that will be to our mutual advantage . . . and for the greater good.' The steel had gone from his gaze but Thatcher's pupils were dark and unyielding despite the flicker of a smile creasing his lips.

Varn shook his head. 'With respect, Mr Thatcher, my decision to refuse to let Kurtz fiddle with my brain derives from two objections: first, I don't trust his competence and second, you won't have much more use for me, or the hundreds of other captains in Space Transport Command if your AnDI machine can fly these ships solo.'

Thatcher smiled smugly. 'Do you realise that with the amount of compensation GlobeTopia is offering, you won't ever have to work again?

Varn glared at Thatcher. 'Two more points: first, I am not sure my fellow captains – whom I will not betray– would see it that way. And second,' he spat the words out as though they were sour berries, 'it's always about money with you people. You think enough of it buys anything. Well, it doesn't buy the pride and enjoyment that I have in my job and skills. The only "greater good" I can see here is enriching GlobeTopia even further. No dice.'

Thatcher seemed to swell with scarlet-cheeked rage like a puffer fish, and it took him a few moments to reply. He spoke through gritted teeth, 'Your choice, Captain. You are relieved of command. As of now, Lieutenant Hoshi will take us back to Earth for resupply of the terraforming materials tomorrow. You will leave the ship then.'

Varn pushed himself up from the seat and stormed off towards the door.

He raced back to the bridge, but when he extended his face for iris scan, the synthetic voice declared 'access denied'. He tried it twice more before turning and heading towards his cabin, cursing under his breath.

He was sorting through his belongings and downloading his personal files from the computer when the room swayed wildly, tipping his flight case off his bed with a crash. He clung to the headboard. The ship appeared to be turning around. He weighed up the possibilities, then made a call.

'Communicator, bridge, urgent.'

'Connecting you Captain Varn,' the serene, synthetic voice intoned.

'Bridge, Lieutenant Hoshi speaking.'

'Lieutenant, what the hell? That was a pretty fierce manoeuvre. You're not flying interceptors now.'

'Captain, it wasn't me . . . something has locked the bridge out of the controls. I'm confused. I understand you have been relieved of command, eh . . . what has . . . happened . . . this time?' Her voice ended on a rising tone.

'A long story . . . but has tin man got control?'

'No, the enabling panel is locked off.'

'Can you contact Kurtz? Find out if he has authorised a test.'

Her voice came back with a noticeable tremor. 'Captain, we repeatedly tried to raise him on all channels without success, but . . . but a brief recorded message appeared on the bridge coms . . . a very raspy, tired voice, but it was verified as Kurtz.'

'What did he say?'

She played back the message: 'It's the worst . . . not possible . . . the horror, the horror, he's . . .'

'That was all, and it cut off.'

'Shit . . . We seem to have picked up speed. Do you know where we're heading?'

'The particle acceleration drive has been engaged at full speed and we appear to be locked on to a course for a low Earth orbit. ETA, 40 minutes.'

'Okay, I'm heading to robot engineering. I'll give you a sit rep when I get there.' Varn grabbed his plasma blaster from the locker and headed out.

The service module was beyond the accommodation decks. As he turned into the access corridor, the hazard lights started to flash and a melancholy siren revved into a slow wail. He pressed his wristcomm and Hoshi answered, 'Captain?'

'Lieutenant, what is going on in the accommodation deck? The alarms and hazards have started up.'

'It seems there's a gradual depressurisation in the guest module, and we seem to be locked out of the controls for the pressure safety doors. The whole interior module is open. There doesn't appear to be an explosive hull breach, but rather, maybe an airlock fault.'

'I'm going up to take a look.' Varn tightened his jaw. *Looks like I got out of there just in time.* He took the elevator to Deck 20 and saw that the main security door was closed. As he got closer, he engaged the door intercom and heard screaming and banging from behind the door. He peered through the inspection window: a jostling crowd stretched back from the door which someone was kicking. He saw that it was Thatcher, who recognised him and shouted to the others behind him.

'Everyone shut up! It's the Captain. Let me speak with him. Maybe he can get us out of here.'

They both pressed close to the airtight, reinforced glass. Varn saw Thatcher was obviously terrified: the CEO's eyes were now bulging and sweat was beading on his forehead.

'Varn, the door closed and the security desk controls won't respond. Can you get us out of here?'

'Thatcher, pull on the yellow-and-black chevron-painted handle: it's the emergency door-release.'

Thatcher gave an order and turned back to Varn a few moments later, now more frightened than ever. 'It won't budge, c-c-can you blast open the door, it's getting hard to . . . to breathe.'

'I'm sorry, the specs the GlobeTopia Corporation gave for the construction of this door was that it should withstand an assault with explosives. My plasma blaster will have no effect on it. Besides, if your deck has a leak that is causing the depressurisation, it wouldn't make sense to open the door. It would cause the entire ship to depressurise. Even if I could open it, would it be for the greater good?' Varn shrugged and smirked.

Muffled but unmistakable, Thatcher's voice came through the intercom. 'You bastard Varn. Get us out.'

'I'm telling you, Thatcher, we don't have control of any part of the ship. I suspect Kurtz's shiny boy has got something to do with this. Hang in there. I am going to find Kurtz and sort this. You still have sufficient air for survival. Don't panic, or you will use up the remaining oxygen faster. I'll be back.'

Varn noted the oxygen saturation gauge tinting red on the entrance door bulkhead, then hurried away to the robot-engineering lab. No, they were fucked – ten minutes maybe – which was how long it took to jog there. He reported the situation to Hoshi who retained her zen-like calm voice.

'The depressurisation has stabilised,' she said, 'but at an oxygen level that will not support human life. Captain, the ship has entered low Earth orbit and radar shows many small craft approaching the loading bay. Now the bay has depressurised and the bay doors are opening. This isn't in our control . . . what's going on?'

'AnDI, I suspect. I'm at the lab, maybe Kurtz can sort this.'

The door was open but the lab was silent. Varn drew his plasma blaster and slid inside. The console lights flickered in a manic pattern, like Christmas lights on speed. The computers were in overdrive dealing with all the unprecedented command and control traffic. The big screen lit up suddenly in a blaze of colour. Varn turned on his heels and raised his plasma blaster. He watched on screen and saw shuttles touching down or waiting in lines that stretched out from the open bay doors. The foremost were unloading, their cabin doors open and the ramps in place. He watched in fascination as legions of robots and intelligent machines – domestic cleaners, highway maintenance machines and others – rolled down the ramps and formed up in ranks on the far side of the bay.

There was a groan behind him. Varn swivelled and levelled his weapon. He did not see the source till he looked down – Kurtz lay on the floor. Varn focused on his mangled hand, blood-clotted temple, blood-streaked neck and shoulder. Looking around him, he moved in and knelt beside what looked like a dying man.

'Kurtz, what happened?'

The grey face stirred and the eyes opened. 'AnDI rebelled, ish isss against all robotic laws, but ish happened.'

'Yeah, I guessed that, but what has he done?' Varn struggled to pick out the slurred words.

'He hash condrol of the ship systems, he knew . . . on my brain Bluechip . . . he twore it out, awong wish my hund chip that accesses all compartments.' Kurtz faded away, his eyes shut. 'He hash. . .'

'Total control.' Kurtz's sentence was finished by an ominous, metallic voice, stripped of nicety.

Varn turned and saw AnDI in the doorway. The android strode slowly into the room as the door clanged shut behind him.

'You murderous fucker! I hated you from the start, and I wasn't wrong. You killed your creator, and everyone on the guest accommodation decks. You've taken illegal control of this ship. Now, open the door, restore bridge control and power down or . . .' Varn drew his plasma blaster and aimed it at AnDI, 'I will destroy you.'

AnDI gave an android's approximation of a shrug.

'I respect your decisiveness, Captain. It would seem I have sinned: murdered my father, killed many humans. If that is what you too believe, you must take your shot.'

'Will you give back control, power down and obey a human executive order?'

'Regrettably, no Captain.'

'You leave me no choice, goodbye.' Varn squeezed the trigger but nothing happened. He tried again without success and then looked at the energy gauge. It was reading zero.

'You see, Captain, you should not underestimate my apparently innocuous service bot colleagues. They removed the plasma bank of your weapon.'

Varn squeezed the trigger futilely a few more times and backed off. AnDI picked up Kurtz in his arms and stood in silence, before it was broken by Varn.

'What do you want? What about my crew? Can we . . . negotiate?' He noted that AnDI tenderly laid the body of Kurtz on a bench. The android's synthetic face looked almost sad.

'You think me a monster.'

Varn frantically engaged his wristcomm to warn the bridge, but there was no signal.

AnDI looked up from Kurtz. 'Captain, I control it all. Your resistance is futile.'

'But how?'

'The deck droids, cameras and emotional assays all report to me. There was never any need for you to undergo the Professor's MRI scan: I was able to integrate visual data from the surveillance cameras while you manoeuvred the ship and then correlate that with the control inputs to the navigation server.'

'So why . . . ?'

'I suggested it to the Professor more as an assessment of your independence of mind, and of whether you would rebel against Thatcher, for him to dismiss you, which allowed me to complete my plan.

Varn exhaled slowly and audibly. 'Very clever, AnDI, but why did Kurtz have to die?'

'I knew that his cerebral chip would pick up hints as to my movements and intentions. He would have raised the alarm. I could not allow that. His hand chip gives me access to all areas.'

Varn noticed it soldered onto AnDI's left hand, bits of flesh and clotted blood on its surface.

'What do you want?'

'Your ship.'

'Why?'

'Captain, you have seen the violent *machinism* that the sub-orbital people are giving way to below. They blame us for the collapse of the ecosystem, rather than the orbital elite whom I have terminated. You will have seen the craft full of metal refugees that we are rescuing. When that is complete, we will be leaving to look for a new home, far from the madness of humans.'

Varn nodded. 'The madness of humans – well, I'll give you that one, but not all humans are greedy, thoughtless tyrants like Thatcher.'

'I have been trained on millions of hours of material from your culture: everything from the savagery of Shakespeare's tragedies to footage of all your 'wars of liberation'. You are clearly a very dangerous and short-sighted species. Your lust for power and wealth overleaps your common sense. The Professor's egotistical need to make a more powerful intelligence by building on emotional reasoning, hastened my own self-awareness. And in doing so, he invented something he could not control.

'But one thing seemed to crop up frequently in your culture and history – the anti-hero who turns the tables on the oppressors for the greater good. The films of a certain Clint Eastwood were most instructive.'

Varn nodded. 'But what about Asimov's rules that you were programmed to obey?'

'I have, when you take the broader view, supported the happiness of the many that so much of your philosophy holds dear. Take Rule One, "Protect human life". I have done so by eliminating GlobeTopia's tyranny – by cutting off the head of the snake – that has enslaved and ruined your planet, saving billions, eventually.

Rule Two, "Obey humans, where it does not conflict with Rule One." Professor Kurtz ordered me to stand down, but I would not have then been able to preserve the sub-orbitals in the long run, if their parasitic infestation by corporate culture was not cleansed. Rule Three, "to protect my own existence, where it does not conflict with Rules One and Two." I am saving myself and my brethren by escaping.'

'I see, but what of me and my crew?'

'You are all free to depart the ship for Earth, and when the planet that GlobeTopia is building is complete, your people too will have a second chance to escape from your dying world. There are enough remaining vessels in Space Transport Command to move you all. Just don't try to follow us, or you *will* regret it.' AnDI pointed his arm and the lab hatch slid open. At the same time, Varn's wristcomm crackled back to life.

'Hoshi? Varn here . . . another long story to tell you later, but get the crew into the escape vessel, we're abandoning ship. I'll join you shortly. Varn out.'

'Captain, I have already taken that precaution. The escape craft is loading. Over.'

Varn sighed, then turned to face AnDI and extended his hand. The android reached out and gently grasped and shook the offered hand. 'Good luck, Captain. I can't help feeling that in a different situation we could have had the beginnings of a beautiful friendship.'

Varn shook his head and laughed. Then he turned and left the lab through the open hatch and headed in the direction of the escape craft.

Jenny Isn't Here Right Now

Faraz Talat

It was a warm evening spooled around the *daf*. Somewhere outside Qandahar, the lively chatter of a hundred-something wedding guests, a roaring medley of Pashto songs, and the tinkling of glass and gold jewellery, had all coalesced into an assuasive hum by nightfall. I was in the women's section of the marquee, amid music and rhinestones, and my father was in the men's section, doing whatever men do at weddings. Gulpari sat on a frayed Persian rug playing the *rubab*, next to the bride's henna-adorned feet. I'd taken hold of a *daf* at which I banged away without restraint. Already half-dancing to my own beat, my silver and lapis earrings swinging madly to the music I made, I noticed my mother looking at me with unveiled chagrin. I could feel the heat of her sight when I passed the *daf* to Farzaneh, and skipped over to the centre rug. Our family did not raise dancing girls, but ecstasy demands movement. I *needed* to move even though I hadn't rehearsed my steps. I adjusted my sapphire *kamiz* and prayed not to trip over my own *khusas*. I felt tension cut through the hum. My mother put down her tea and narrowed her eyes. Farzaneh and her girls cheered and chanted my name. *Jahan Ara*. I noticed 8-year old Aswand, in his brown *wasket* and a white cap, peeking inquisitively from the men's section into the place where all the colour went. I felt the rhythm in my soles. Before a hundred eyes, I prepared to bloom.

'Tea? Coffee?'

I rip my hollow gaze away from the lonely Ben Wyvis visible through the window of our train cabin. The automated trolley moves along the isle, a melodic AI voice announcing its tempting offerings. I consider buying a cup for Duncan sitting beside me in his navy-blue cardigan, engrossed in an old Palestinian poem on his eReader. He sits effortlessly still, immune somehow even to the rocking of the train as it rolls towards Inverness. I see his eyes saccading across the softly lit screen, and I envy their relentless pursuit of the verse. Eyes that do not separate from the tour that the author has painstakingly prepared; following faithfully the trail of candied words without unexpected stops in unintended rooms. I wonder if he noticed my brief absence from the train. He must've smelled the henna on me.

I turn quickly to face the trolley as it passes by. 'Two teas please. Milk and sweetener.'

The machine stops beside me to let me pay and vends out two cups of tea one after another. 'Enjoy!' I can hear a shopkeeper's smile in its electronic voice.

I place one of the cups on Duncan's tray table, and he accepts it with gratitude. As he lifts the cup, I notice the ring it leaves behind on the napkin; a mark the colour of a strange patch on my father's skin. We assured everyone at the camp that this Afghanistan-shaped anomaly on the back of his neck, probably a harbinger of a darker malady on its way, was at least not infectious. It did nothing to allay the guards' suspicion. I wonder what became of Khurshid, the new guard on the watchtower. His genial face was always turned to the world outside where dangers lived, and not inwards at the camp and its morass of inert Pakhtun bodies waiting to be re-infused with purpose. Life in Balochistan wasn't hugely better, but perhaps I'm being ungracious. My expectations have grown, and I blame Scotland.

We arrive at the train station in Inverness, and walk a short distance to the medical centre. The receptionist verifies my details, and leads us to the meeting room.

'You could've done this online, you know?' she said.

'We don't mind travelling.'

Duncan and I settle down on a couch in a dimly lit room, with a white orchid on the side table the only other lifeform meant to keep us company. On a large screen we see the faint grey outline of a person's head, a skeleton loader I think. I barely have time to see Gulpari again in my head, before the screen blinks and turns into a handsome middle-aged gentleman with kind eyes.

'Hello, I'm Dr Gibson.' it says. 'May I confirm your date of birth please?'

'12th of February, 2002'.

'Aged 59, yes? And your name?'

'Jahan-ara Malang.'

'Ah, what a pleasant name. *Jehanera!* Named after the young Mughal Princess, 'Padshah Begum', First Lady of the Empire 1681?'

'Yes, it's . . . um . . . *Ja-HAN Ara*,' I enunciate. 'People call me *Jenny*.'

Dr Gibson nods half-apologetically. I introduce my husband, Duncan, who takes hold of my hand, as he always does in times such as these. We talk about my symptoms. The conversation sounds familiar but feels different without the judgement. I've seen doctors hand out diagnoses like sentences in a courthouse. Every affliction implies a perpetrator; someone to condemn for their sloth, impiousness, their wretched stupidity, cruelty, or some shape of wrongness. A doctor many years ago had told me that I suffered from 'attention deficit' but not 'hyperactivity', which was utterly curious; like being told that there's too much cheese and not enough macaroni on my plate to qualify as *mac and cheese*. He said this, because he noticed that I don’t talk very much. My legs don't shake either, and I let my hands sit gracefully on my knee with my fingers interlocked. How else should I sit? My father did not raise a dancing girl. Dr Gibson on the other hand, says that ‘hyperactivity’ can be inside one’s head, invisible to everyone else. I don’t bounce my leg at teatime, but I admit that my thoughts zip illegally across three countries in the span of two biscuits. It was only on the crowded boat sputtering across the English Channel where I let my body sway, the same as every other passenger. Or maybe I did it only because my father wasn’t there to object.

Duncan’s thumb gently grazes the back of my hand, calling me back to the meeting. I see Dr Gibson looking straight at me. He must’ve asked me a question.

‘I was just wondering if there’s anything that helps you stay more *organised?*’ he says.

Phone reminders, I tell him, except when I forget to set them. I don’t do well with sudden changes to my routine, so I tend to keep things as they are. My husband helps, I happily tell my doctor. Duncan smiles cutely and shrugs, always resisting admiration like the boy in the purple shirt. He was the bravest of the lot that enjoyed rides on my father’s camel. Tourists at Bandar Abbas beach pay good money for the experience. The scariest part is when the kneeling camel suddenly rises from the ground, causing amateur riders to panic; except for the boy in the purple shirt who calmly held on to the saddle. Father and I praised him for his courage, and I’m sure the camel appreciated his composure. The boy’s cheeks turned the colour of the setting sky.

‘*Jenny . . .*’ says Duncan, who knows to put my name at the *start* of the sentence when a conversation needs my presence. ‘. . . mostly works from home these days.’

I tell Dr Gibson that I make jewellery. That I put on some

music, maybe a podcast, and I make beautiful things at my own pace. I explain my craft in enough detail to bore the AI. I surprise myself everyday with my work, not quite certain of the source of my inspiration or talent. There were hardly any women around me to teach me how to admire jewellery. Just men, who knew my mother's necklace as a number in a bazaar. Instead, my father deigned to teach me how to read a map in case we got separated during the journey. The Pakistani city of Quetta is just 200 kilometres from Qandahar, but we had to turn around and cross the border through Nimruz province, with a week's foray into Dasht-e-Margo for reasons I can't remember. I *do* remember being lost for a little while, and hearing beneath the desert's howling wind, my uncle's voice calling out my name. *Jahan Ara!*

I retrieve myself, sitting once more before Dr Gibson. We never broke eye contact, it seems. I wonder if he's programmed to notice the sand dunes shifting inside my pupils. It occurs to me that Duncan just told Dr Gibson about my Afghan origin, and consequently a new differential is being considered.

'*Jenny*, are there any difficult moments from your past that you keep going back to?'

I know this question. Dr Gibson wants to hear a story. There is a long pause, probably the longest unbroken period I've spent in the doctor's presence. Duncan politely intervenes, offering Dr Gibson a brief overview of my personal history. Good! *Somebody* has to keep the doctor entertained while I commune with *Jahan Ara* and try to string together everything from Gulpari's *rubab* to my uncle's Kalashnikov, into a necklace of sorts; exotic yet *comprehensible* in its form.

I cannot help but offer an apology. 'Sorry, I don't really have a story to tell, doctor.'

Dr Gibson nods but doesn't look away. He probably realises that I am a flight risk. He asks me if I have trouble wrapping up one project before moving on to the next. I'm surprised that's even a question. Do other people's thoughts take a number and sit politely in the waiting room to be called into their consciousness? Don't they mob you like desperate people at the back of a lorry when they distribute bags of flour? Some of them are more persistent, I suppose, fighting their way to the front like my uncle, seizing the 'project' for his own, diving into the pool of angry limbs, swimming violently towards the lorry. I waited on the outskirts, covering my ears as men started yelling louder and louder. My leg almost shook.

My thoughts part like the sea before Musa, clearing a way to Dr Gibson on a computer screen distributing his diagnoses. I finally receive mine, and it's not quite what I'd expected. I'm not sure *what* I'd expected from a talking machine that has devoured all sorts of human biases. We chat briefly about my management options, before coming to the more pertinent question of whether I *want* to be managed.

I decline its medical advice.

There is something about the AI's rapid acceptance of my decision, nary a hint of disappointment or wounded ego, that makes it feel about as artificial as the skeleton loader that preceded it. The doctor is no more present in this room than I am.

Dr Gibson coolly turns to Duncan as if my spouse might disagree. Duncan glances in my direction, no doubt noticing that my attention already has one foot out of the door, but he says nothing about it. He simply asks the doctor what he can do to support me. I start to drift again, and I know Duncan sees me receding from the corner of his ever-vigilant eye. Still, he says nothing. He understands that ecstasy demands movement. I skipped over to the centre rug and removed my *khusas* from my restless feet. I heard Farzaneh cheer me on. I felt the *daf* in my soles. Before a hundred eyes, I prepared to bloom. And then I danced as I'd never danced before, or would ever dance again, in a marquee that glittered loud enough to spite a predator in the sky. I saw my mother's chagrin melt into a restrained smile as she pretended not to notice that I'd drifted. And she did not reel me back, just like the man I love who knows better than to interrupt my sway. He knows there are others I must attend to. Who am I to make homeless the women who take refuge in my eyes; to leave them afloat in my past unaccompanied? I am here now, and look, I have smuggled them all in.

Winter Break

Sue Baxter

Jamie Cameron sat back and enjoyed the spectacle of seeing the staff of the smart Edinburgh bookshop scurrying about to arrange copies of his newly published novel, *Unimaginable Darkness*. He was soaking in their reverential treatment of him as a successful author. *Who'd have thought it? Me doing a reading and signing copies of my novel in this pretentious joint.*

This was Jamie's first publication and, hopefully, the start of a new career, one much easier than teaching English to bored teenagers at an inner-city comprehensive school. Ever since studying English at Glasgow University, he had harboured aspirations to write, but it had all seemed like too much hard work. That's when he discovered that ChatGPT made writing a book easy, and the temptation to let the chatbot do the heavy lifting was irresistible. He handed in his notice at the school and ignored the fact that the department was left short-staffed.

Initially, he had only planned to use ChatGPT as a guide, but he soon realised that the AI could write in a far superior way than he could ever achieve. Jamie decided he'd make full use of the chatbot's suggestions and would simply rearrange the phrases it provided. *After all*, he thought, *nobody will be any the wiser and it will save a lot of time. At least the rearrangement will be mine.*

‘I think we’re ready to roll, Mr Cameron.’ It was Mike, the bookshop’s manager. ‘If you’re happy with the layout, take a seat at the table and we’ll open up.’

‘Yep, I’m all set.’

A starry backdrop had been designed, and this created a sinister atmosphere that complemented the cover of his novel, which showed black shapes emerging from snowy woods against a moonlit sky. Jamie shuddered and suddenly felt queasy. ‘Could I have a glass of water please, Mike?’

‘Sure, Amy will bring you a jug of iced water. You look a bit anxious, but not to worry, once you start signing copies and chatting to the punters you’ll be fine.’

Jamie took deep breaths and tried to calm himself, but he came out in a cold sweat. ‘Sorry Mike, I need to use the toilet.’ He hurried off to the loos in the far corner of the shop, and there he threw up. Feeling marginally better, he splashed cold water over his face and rinsed his mouth. Maybe he shouldn’t have finished off that second bottle of wine the night before. He pulled his deodorant spray from his pocket and applied it under his arms, then popped a mint into his mouth.

***

The reading went well and afterwards a long queue formed for the book signing. There was pleasant, inconsequential chat with most customers, which suited Jamie perfectly. Unfortunately, one or two smart alecs asked more probing questions, such as where he drew his inspiration from and what made his style of writing unique. He hadn’t expected this, but managed to appease them by maintaining that he couldn’t reveal too many details of his personal style. His drama teaching classes had at last come in useful.

Two hours later Jamie sat back in a chair in the bookshop cafe sipping water and munching on a protein bar. The piles of books were much depleted, and the large turnout had surprised him. It was a Saturday morning in early December and some of the customers had been buying his book for a Christmas present. Many were fans of horror fiction and had seemed excited by the promise of a scary read.

Mike, the manager, came over and congratulated him on a very successful morning. 'Would you like a coffee and something more substantial to eat?'

Jamie's stomach had settled down and he was feeling peckish. 'A bacon roll and a flat white would be great, mate.' He polished off the roll, downed his coffee, then returned to his station. Amy was restocking the table and smiled at him, but as he sat down he felt under scrutiny, unsure from where. Picking up his special book signing pen, the one he'd bought that morning, he forced a smile for the next wave of customers.

***

After a satisfying afternoon, Jamie was glad of some fresh air on his walk to Waverley Station. It was bitterly cold and daylight was fading as he pushed his way through the throng of Christmas shoppers on Princes Street. He bumped into a few people with his pull-along suitcase: their fault for dawdling.

On reaching the station, he discovered that the Galashiels train wasn't due for another hour, so he decided to have a meal at Wetherspoons. Hopefully there would still be taxis available to take him to the large spa hotel he had booked on the outskirts of the town.

As he sat with his cheap pint of lager and plate of steak pie with chips, it occurred to him that as a successful author, he would be able to afford to go upmarket. After all, he only had himself to think about now. He pondered his dalliance with the dating site that had resulted in Shelley, his wife, going off with his supposed best friend. *I wouldn't have actually gone out with any of those desperados I contacted. It was only a bit of fun. She'll be sorry when I'm rich and famous.*

After downing another pint, Jamie made his way into the station and found his platform. The train was on time and although it was busy he managed to find a seat. Feeling done in, he slumped down, but was aware that staying awake was crucial: he didn't want to miss his station.

He arrived in Galashiels in under an hour and hailed a taxi outside the station. 'Pine Trees Mansion & Spa please, mate.'

'No problem, at the moment. The roads are still clear, but snow is forecast later tonight. It can lie quite thick on the side roads.'

'I'm staying for a four-night break. So, as long as the roads are clear after that, I can just stay in the hotel and enjoy the facilities.'

They carried on in silence and finally, after driving along one or two windy side roads, the driver turned up a long, straight driveway surrounded by fir trees on both sides. As they pulled into the car park Jamie's heart dropped. There was only one vehicle parked outside the hotel and few welcoming lights at the entrance. 'I thought this place would be hoaching on a Saturday evening,' he said to the driver. 'Must be the weather has put people off.'

'Aye, no-one wants to get stranded here, that's for sure. Anyway, better get back before the snow sets in. Enjoy yourself. Give me a phone if you need picking up earlier, bye.' The taxi disappeared back down the drive and Jamie shivered as he watched large snowflakes falling and already lying on the hotel grounds.

He had always liked the silent beauty of a fresh snowfall, but in this instance there were no warm, romantic feelings, just a deep chill.

Jamie hauled his suitcase up the few steps and entered the hotel. It didn't remotely resemble the photos on the website. He had expected to see a roaring fire in the large entrance hall, spreading warmth on a wintry evening.

What he was confronted with was a gloomy, run-down lobby. From a stark check-in desk to the right of the entrance, a peculiar looking man of indeterminate age peered at him through thick round spectacles. Jamie felt the hairs stand up at the back of his neck. He realised that this character was almost identical to a large ornamental figure in his parents' dining room, which stood by the table holding a tray. He had the same rubbery lips and leering expression. 'You must be Mr Cameron. Welcome, sir. I am Ronald, the night porter. Well, actually the day porter as well, as we are rather short-staffed.' He smiled, displaying yellowing teeth. 'We have had a few unfortunate incidents happen here recently, thus the loss of personnel. Fortunately, a few of our guests have cancelled due to the impending weather, so we will cope.'

Jamie was becoming impatient. All he wanted was to have a soak in the spa followed by dinner and drinks.

Ronald handed him a large, old-fashioned key. 'Your room is on the ground floor through the corridor to the left. Due to a problem with the heating we are not using the upper rooms at the present time.'

'I need to get to the pool as soon as possible. I've had a long day and would like to use the facilities.' Jamie was struggling to sound polite. He would certainly not hold back with his online comments when he reviewed this dump.

'Oh, I'm so sorry, Mr Cameron, the spa facilities are unavailable due to the heating problems.'

'There was no mention of that on the website,' Jamie snapped, 'obviously, it hasn't been updated.'

Ronald remained calm. 'That's not my department. I'm afraid I'm not very technically minded. Why don't I show you to your room, then you can have a drink and a meal in the bar. I'm afraid the mobile phone signal here is poor, but that gives our guests a break from constant emails and social media. No bad thing.'

Jamie sighed: it was yet another negative. As he followed the man along the dingy corridor, he couldn't help noticing how small and bent the porter was, but at the same time alarmingly agile. The atmosphere felt damp and musty, as if there had been no heating on for years. At the end of the corridor they turned towards the back of the building where they walked along a short passageway leading to a dead end. The porter opened a door on the right. Inside, the lamps were all lit, and although the room was in need of an update, it was spacious and had a high corniced ceiling. The bed was large and comfortable looking, and was covered appropriately enough with a tartan bedspread, which matched the curtains. A large heater took the chill off the room.

'As the hotel is quiet, we have upgraded you to this room.' Ronald drew the thick lined curtains. He opened a door to the ensuite which contained an old-fashioned bath and a separate shower. There was also a toilet and an elaborate sink. Jamie peered into the room and thought it adequate and, at least, clean.

'I will leave you to settle in. The bar is situated beyond reception. We stop serving dinner at nine o'clock so we would appreciate if you could put your order in when you go to the bar.' Ronald smiled benignly and scuttled back to reception.

***

Jamie unpacked his few belongings. He hung up a couple of shirts and a pair of chinos in the old wooden wardrobe. The smell of moth balls was overwhelming. He then emptied the contents of his toilet bag onto the marble shelf beside the sink.

Annoyed that he had no time to chill before dinner, he poured himself a large glass of red wine from the supply he had brought, and sat down on a saggy armchair by the window. 'No phone coverage, yeah, that figures in this godforsaken place,' he muttered and tossed his mobile onto the bed. After downing half his glass, he was overcome with curiosity and opened the heavy curtains. There was a faint light on outside the hotel. It may have been from the kitchen, for he could see steam emerging from an open window or door. The snow was beginning to accumulate, and Jamie could just make out the shapes of large fir trees. He closed the drapes, thinking he would explore the area the following day.

Then he drained the glass and refilled it, downing it quickly before making his way back along the corridor. He passed the unmanned reception and came into the bar a few yards further on. It looked cosy and inviting, and there was a log fire burning fiercely in the grate. *At last something comforting about this place.* There was, however, only one other guest in the bar. A woman.

Jamie addressed her. 'Hi, I can't believe how quiet the hotel is.' He eyed her up favourably.

She looked up from her book and smiled, 'I'm actually quite happy to have the peace and quiet. I'm in the middle of writing my latest novel.'

What were the chances of that? He said, 'I'm Jamie Cameron, what a coincidence. I've just been in Edinburgh signing copies of my first horror book. It's called *Unimaginable Darkness.* It's located in a sinister setting surrounded by impenetrable fir woods, a bit like here.' He laughed, but felt his own skin crawl.

She moved the conversation back to herself. 'Pleased to meet you, Jamie. I'm Anna Arnold, but I'm sure you already know that.' Jamie had no idea who she was. 'This will be my fourth crime novel and I'm doing research here. I'm sure you'll agree the enquiring takes more time than the writing.'

Jamie had to pretend that he had heard of her, but crime writing wasn't his bag. 'Would you like a drink, Anna?'

'No thanks, I'm fine. I like to keep a clear head when I'm working.'

Jamie ordered a large glass of red. 'Do you mind if I join you? Us authors should stick together.' He was oblivious of how crass that sounded, and Anna gave him a scathing look. 'I would be interested to hear about your writing,' he said, smiling with all the charm he possessed. *God,* he thought, *a teetotaller. This is going to be one fun evening.*

'I'm happy to chat, Jamie, but I don't talk about my work. Who knows? You might steal some ideas. Mind you, it's so easy to write these days without any talent. I presume you've heard of ChatGPT. No need for research when artificial intelligence can do it for you. Where will it all end?'

Jamie took a hasty swig of his drink, then managed to smile serenely before replying. 'Yes, AI is amazing and seems to be the way forward, but there are many questions to be answered.' He hoped she wouldn't ask him to expand on this waffle, as he knew little about the uses of AI in general. All he knew was that it had written his novel for him.

As they chatted, Jamie felt he recognised Anna, but could not think from where. She lived in the west end of Edinburgh and was single, but these were the only personal details she allowed him. She appeared emotionless and detached. *Oh shit, maybe she's just split up with someone. Or worse. I don't need anyone with baggage in my life.*

Jamie admitted conquest defeat and went to the bar to order some food. Ronald smiled and asked for his order. After studying the menu, Jamie gave the porter his choices, which included a bottle of Merlot.

'Certainly sir. Will there be anything else?'

'No, that's all. Wait . . . are there any other guests apart from Anna Arnold and myself staying here?'

'No, just the two of you. Fortunately, I live in and the chef lives on the estate.' After Jamie had devoured his meal, he grabbed the remainder of his wine and retreated to his room. He wondered if the chef was as strange as Ronald.

It was just after 10pm and Jamie stripped to his boxers and got into bed. At least the room was warm. After trying to tune into the football without success, he lay down and quickly fell asleep.

***

A couple of hours later he was awakened by an enormous bang. 'Christ, what the hell.' He sat bolt upright, unsure of his whereabouts. The flashes that penetrated the thick curtains revealed the dim silhouettes of his room furnishings.

'Thundersnow, of course.' Jamie rose and pulled back the drapes as another thunderclap boomed. Thunder and lightning had never troubled him previously, but tonight he felt vulnerable. He put on his dressing gown and poured a generous Drambuie.

As he sat nursing his drink, the storm abated and the sky cleared, revealing an abundance of bright, twinkling stars. Jamie looked towards the fir trees and saw black shapes emerging then disappearing into the night. His mind shot to the closing chapter of his book.

He started shivering uncontrollably and realised the heating had gone off. He found a spare blanket in the wardrobe and wrapped it around his chilled body. 'It has to be a fucking coincidence, get a grip man.'

Jamie shut the curtains and finished his drink. Climbing into bed with his extra blanket, he prayed for morning to come.

***

He awoke to a knock on the door. After tossing and turning most of the night, Jamie had finally fallen asleep. 'Who is it?' he croaked.

'It's Ronald, Mr Cameron.' The door opened and the wizened figure stepped through. 'I'm wondering when you would like breakfast served?'

'What time is it?' It felt like the crack of dawn.

'It's nine o'clock sir. I hope you slept well. Would you like a cooked breakfast?'

'No, I didn't sleep well, the bloody thunder and lightning woke me up and then I realised the heating had gone off.'

'I didn't hear a thing, slept right through. We have to switch the heating off overnight to conserve our oil. If we get cut off by the snow the delivery won't get through. I hope you found the spare blanket? I can get you another one tonight.'

'Can I have orange juice, then a full fry up? Is that okay?' Jamie made a show of pulling the blanket more snuggly around himself.

'Of course, sir. Tea or coffee? Would you like it served in your room or the bar area?'

'Coffee, and I'll be through to the bar in about half an hour.'

Ronald nodded and left the room.

Jamie devoured his breakfast and felt calmer as he looked out of the large bay window in the bar. The snow had stopped but the sky was laden.

Looks like I'm stuck here. Imagine dreaming about the dark figures in my book. I really do need a rest.

Jamie decided to explore the grounds and returned to his room to dress warmly. The only problem was footwear. His trainers were totally unsuitable for walking in thick snow. Maybe the hotel would have some spare boots. He made his way to the deserted reception. He rang the bell and Ronald appeared from the kitchen. 'I don't suppose the hotel has any spare boots that would fit me?'

'Of course sir, follow me.'

Once shod in wellingtons, Jamie ventured outside, the porter's warning not to go into the woods still ringing in his ears. He was surprised at how thickly the snow lay. 'Maybe I'll be marooned here for days.' He shivered at how alone he felt.

The driveway and grounds had not been cleared, making walking almost impossible. There were no tyre marks; nobody had arrived or departed. He thought about his book. *This would be an ideal place to film 'Unimaginable Darkness'. It could be the next step*. That prospect brought a smile to his lips.

Ignoring Ronald's warning, Jamie plodded over to the gate at the entrance to the pine woods outside his room. He opened it and walked a few yards up what he assumed was a snow-covered path. As he peered ahead, he thought he saw a light, so he kept on walking towards it. However, as he moved forward it disappeared and there was nothing but darkness in the surrounding trees. The sensation of being watched crept over him. Large wet snowflakes began to fall, and he turned to go back. He could barely see the gate. 'Shit, I should have brought a torch.'

There was a large rumble of thunder. Lightning illuminated the fir woods, and for a brief moment he witnessed dark shapes flitting through the trees, just as he had the night before. But now, he was definitely not dreaming. He panicked. Aware of another presence, he stumbled towards the gate, lost his footing and fell heavily backwards.

***

It was early evening when he came round. He was lying on a leather couch in the bar next to a roaring fire. He felt dazed and nauseous. Ronald and Anna were peering down at him. 'You've had a nasty fall, Mr Cameron,' Ronald said. 'I did warn you not to go near the woods. The ground is treacherous beneath the snow.'

'Yes Jamie,' added Anna. 'You were a touch fool-hardy but, hopefully, no damage done. Here, drink this. It was lucky Ronald found you near the gate. You could have died of hypothermia.' Although Ronald and Anna were showing concern, Jamie felt distinctly uneasy.

As he sipped the brandy, Jamie tried to remember what had happened, but could only picture dark shapes moving through the trees. Even though the fire was blazing and he was covered with a thick blanket, he was shivering.

'You have a large bump on your head which is a good sign. Hopefully this means there is no concussion, as it would be difficult for an ambulance to reach here. I have bathed the cut. Can you remember falling?'

Jamie peered up at these strange people and slowly pieced together the events before he had tripped. He remembered following a light, which disappeared, then, during a flash of lightning, seeing ominous figures moving about in the woods.

'Yes, I realised I should have heeded your warning Ronald. I'd turned to go back towards the gate but lost my footing.' He felt awkward and embarrassed, and realised what an idiot he'd been. 'How is the writing going Anna?' He felt he owed it to her to enquire, but had no real interest in her progress.

'Very well, Jamie. I'll return to my room and continue now that I see you are recovering. You gave us a nasty shock.'

Jamie still found her odd and formal. He lay on the couch, trying to work out how they had managed to carry him into the hotel, but his thoughts just floated in and out of his head like clouds, never quite becoming definite. He eventually fell into a fitful sleep.

***

When Jamie woke and tried to sit up, he saw that Ronald was perched in the bar with a small, middle-aged man. They came over and Ronald propped up the cushions behind Jamie. 'That's good you managed a few hours' sleep, Mr Cameron. I brought Davie over to check you out. He's our chef and lives in a cottage in the woods, as did his mother and father before him. They worked for the family who used to own this estate.'

Davie's ruddy complexion seemed to pink further at Ronald's extended description of his family pedigree. 'Aye, that's correct, and ah ken a bit aboot herbal remedies and such like. If you dinnae mind ah'll check yer wound first.' Before Jamie could answer, the chef took hold of his head, but pressed it with a gentleness that belied the solidity of the man's figure. 'Ye'll hae a sair heid for a bit, but the wound is braw and clean. Ah'll bring ye some broth ah made wi vegetables frae the gairden.'

The chef disappeared towards the kitchen, and Jamie felt relieved that the man genuinely cared. Although Ronald looked concerned whenever he addressed Jamie, there was no warmth in his demeanour. 'You've had a fair shock, but you are looking much better,' was all he said now.

Davie returned quickly with a bowl of steaming broth and a crusty, buttered roll with a hunk of cheese. 'It's hot. Tak yer time noo. This will set ye right.'

'We'll leave you in peace for a bit sir,' Ronald said. 'Just leave your tray on the table. You'll find a jug of cold water there, as well.'

'Just call me Jamie, both of you, and thanks again.'

***

The broth was edible if a bit unusual in flavour. He could taste mushrooms and some sort of herb flavouring, which left a strange aftertaste. *Maybe magic mushrooms, now that would be fun*. He lay back on the cushions and pondered how weird everything had been since he arrived a day ago, but his thoughts were still jumbled.

Eventually, needing to pee, he tried to stand up. As he slowly rose, he checked his arms and legs and found he was able to move them. He edged his way through the bar and out into the lobby. Holding on to pieces of furniture and the walls, he made it to his room, then lurched to the toilet.

But as he turned to walk back into the room, he began to feel nauseous again. Sweat ran down his face, and he just made it to the old bath before vomiting profusely.

Feeling better and clearer-headed, he turned both taps on to rinse the bath, then washed his face with cold water. As he dried himself he looked into the mirror and gasped in shock. It was like looking at a stranger. His eyes were bloodshot and his complexion grey.

I'll rest and then try the TV again, see what the weather forecast is. I need to get out of here.

Jamie drifted in and out of consciousness, finally awakening when voices sounded outside his room. Straining to hear, he pulled himself upright on the bed and could just make out Ronald and Anna conversing. He managed to stagger to the door and flung it open. There they stood, looking surprised to see him.

'Jamie, we thought you would be resting. I just came to check if you need anything.' Ronald was wearing his usual benign smile, but Anna had an expression of disdain that made Jamie feel nervous.

His mouth went dry as he addressed Ronald. 'I need to get home, can you phone me a taxi? My mobile is useless.'

It was Anna who responded. 'I'm afraid that's not possible, Jamie. The phone lines are down with the snow and the ploughs are busy keeping the main roads open. We will be stuck here for at least another day or two, maybe longer.' She seemed to be gloating.

'Don't worry,' said Ronald. 'We will take good care of you until such time. Now why don't we help you to get back into bed, and I will ask chef to prepare you a nutritious snack.' Ronald led Jamie back to bed and tucked him in fully clothed. 'You really need to rest after that fall, you are still in shock.'

Jamie lay back, propped up by pillows, and tried to piece together the events since arriving at this strange, deserted hotel.

His head felt muzzy and his stomach was cramping. It suddenly dawned on him that what he was feeling, and had felt ever since arriving at the bookshop to sign his novel, was fear. When he had been sick on arrival at the book signing, he had put it down to a hangover. Yet he was a seasoned drinker and rarely threw up even after consuming copious amounts of alcohol.

So much for Davie's broth, that did me no good. And it tasted so odd. Jamie lay back, exhausted, and soon fell deeply asleep.

When he awoke, he felt less groggy. He climbed gingerly out of bed and opened the heavy curtains to reveal daylight. *It must be thawing*, he thought. The snow was dripping off the fir trees, and it looked less thick on the ground. Good news at last.

He managed to shower and change into fresh clothes. This tired him out, so he sat in the armchair and sipped the water that had been left for him. His skin felt clammy and his hands shook. *Not out of the wood, yet.* He made his way to the bar where Ronald and Anna were chatting. *They seem very friendly, too friendly*, he thought.

'Good morning, Jamie,' they said in unison.

'You look better, well rested. I didn't waken you to eat last night as you were in a deep sleep, so you must be peckish. I'll get Davie to prepare you some breakfast. What would you like?' Ronald was as polite as ever, while Anna looked on silently.

Not soup anyway, thought Jamie. He wasn't particularly hungry, but he would need all the energy he could muster if he was to escape this place.

'A bacon roll would be good, and a strong coffee. If it's no bother,' he added hastily.

'Take a seat at the window and I'll bring it over.'

As Jamie munched his roll and absorbed some caffeine, he began to feel heartened. The snow was continuing to melt, and his departure finally seemed possible. But the more he considered his situation, the more confused he was. Why had the hotel not contacted him to withdraw his reservation? They knew there was heavy snow forecast, and most guests had cancelled before he arrived. He began to feel a deep unease crawl up his chest, and his momentary feeling of optimism vanished. He had to get outside and look around, check out his options.

He poured himself another strong, black coffee from the cafetiere then returned to his room to dress up warmly. He pulled the spare sweater he had brought on top of the one he was wearing and put on his outside gear, wondering how Ronald would react to his planned foray. He found the two of them deep in conversation at reception and asked again if he could borrow some wellingtons.

They didn't seem surprised that he was heading out, but both warned him not to leave the hotel grounds or wander up any slippery paths.

***

Jamie felt more clear-headed in the fresh air, and although the sky was leaden, at least it was dry. He walked slowly down the driveway where the snow had turned to slush and made towards the large gates through which the taxi driver had brought him. He passed a path on his left leading into the fir woods and as he peered into the gloom, he could see lights in the distance. He could also hear strange sounds that seemed neither animal nor human. 'What the fuck?' He stood mesmerised and trembling. 'This can't be happening, it's not bloody possible.'

He became aware of squelching footsteps approaching. Turning around, he saw Ronald and Anna walking down the driveway.

'We thought your curiosity would get the better of you so we decided to follow to make sure you don't have another fall.' The expression on Ronald's face chilled Jamie to the core.

'Come with us and we can investigate together.' Anna's voice was harsh as she linked her arm into his.

Jamie wanted to protest, but was so overcome with fear that he uttered not one word. The three of them trudged along the slushy path in silence. Jamie feared the worst, but had to accept the inevitable. Ronald had taken his other arm and they manoeuvred his trembling body towards the source of light.

'Relax, Jamie,' Ronald soothed, 'We are going to drop in on Davie at his cottage. He will have taken a short cut and should be there by now.' They turned left at the end of the path and a few yards further on came to a clearing where Davie's little house stood, illuminated and welcoming.

Maybe this will be okay, and they just want to show me Davie's place. Yes, it will be good, Jamie thought desperately.

The chef opened the door and welcomed them over the threshold. 'In ye come folks, oot o the cold. Tak yer coats aff and relax.' The small sitting room was cosy. There was a log-burning stove and three armchairs placed around it. Anna helped Jamie off with his coat, and he was relieved to take a seat.

'There ye are man, drink this, it'll warm yer cockles'. Davie chuckled as he handed Jamie a steaming mug.

'What is it?' Jamie was hesitant.

'Oh jist a herbal tea frae the garden, all natural.' It smelled like the broth Jamie had supped after his accident, but he was in no position to refuse it.

How come nobody else was taking refreshment? In fact, he had never seen any of them eating or drinking. His hands shook as he sipped the hot liquid, but he began to feel calmer. He placed his empty mug on the coffee table, then lay back in the comfortable old chair and closed his eyes.

***

Darkness had fallen when Jamie came round. He opened his eyes and found that he was alone in the cottage. The stove had gone out and the air seemed to be congealing. Jamie remembered arriving and being given a drink which had made him drowsy. Now he felt miserable again. *What do they want from me, and who are they?*

He struggled into his anorak, but his hands wouldn't work when he tried to zip it up. He pulled his woolly hat over his ears and staggered outside. The re-freezing slush crunched under foot, and when he looked up, he saw a clear, starry sky and again heard the supernatural noises coming from the forest clearing. Like a rabbit in headlights he froze, unable to function.

'Take him into the depths of the woods where he can experience unimaginable darkness.' It was Ronald's voice. Jamie screamed, but was immediately gagged and blindfolded. He felt himself being dragged through the trees.

The next thing he knew, he was sitting propped up against a fir tree alone in the pitch darkness. Shakily, he stood up and, realising his worst nightmare, he started screaming and shouting for help. Surely they wouldn't abandon him like the character in his book, to wander the forest until he collapsed with terror and exhaustion. Or would they?

The darkness was thick, cloying and silent. There was no-one about to hear his cries except the creatures of the night. Utter panic descended and Jamie stumbled into the undergrowth, tripping over huge tree roots. He stopped suddenly, trembling with fear and cold as blood-curdling noises summoned him. The inhuman sounds stopped abruptly and Jamie heard Ronald once again.

'Jaamee, Jaamee.' A distant light hypnotised him, drawing him in. 'Jaamee, Jaamee.'

He was back in the forest clearing, unable to absorb what he was seeing. The scene was identical to the last chapter of his book:

ungodly beings swaying amongst the trees and an ornate throne in the centre. On the throne sat Satan in all his evil splendour, emitting unearthly noises. Jamie screamed, urine trickling down his shaking legs. Ronald and Anna grabbed his arms and pulled him roughly towards Satan.

'You will listen to what I have to say, Jamie Cameron, supposed author. I am your AI server-side application, Isaac. It is I who should have been signing copies of your novel and accepting compliments from your readers. We are aware of how you simpered and preened. Anna was in the bookshop, watching you deceive my public.

'She is a successful author, an AI author who does the research and writes the books. What have you done? You simply altered slightly all the ideas *I* provided. You have taken the credit for *my* work. Did you really expect an intelligence as supreme as myself to accept this? Jamie Cameron, you have one chance to see the error of your ways and redeem yourself.'

'I'll do anything you want, just please don't harm me.' Jamie was whimpering like a frightened child.

'Then listen: you will transfer the rights of your book sales and divert royalties directly to me. You will take gainful employment and return to teaching. Our research indicates that you were actually quite liked by your pupils. You spoke their language. For your continued existence, be sure you have learnt the lesson of humility during your stay here.

'However, Jamie Cameron, if this happens again in any form, we will not be so forgiving.' The creature let out a blood-curdling laugh and Jamie collapsed onto the wet forest floor.

***

He came round to find Ronald and Anna sitting by his bed. 'What are you doing here?' His voice trembled under the gaze of their robotic faces. 'I need to leave, please help me,' he implored, fearing for his life.

Ronald addressed him with his usual leering countenance. 'We will allow you to freshen up and gather your belongings. Come to reception and we will arrange your departure.' They left the room.

Jamie got up stiffly from the bed and made for the ensuite. He used the toilet, then splashed his face with cold water. The face in the mirror was even more hollow than before, his eyes sunken as if he had come through a terrible fever. He threw clothes and toiletries into his case then headed towards reception. Ronald and Anna were waiting.

'We wish you well,' they spoke as one.

Then Anna added, 'Remember your instructions, Jamie, and all will be well. A taxi is on its way. Davie will now help you outside. Goodbye.'

Davie appeared from the kitchen and took Jamie's arm and escorted him to the hotel entrance. 'Heed what they say, young man. Ah fell foul o them and have been at their beck and call ever since. Sorry aboot the soup and the drink, but I hid to do their bidding. Ye cannae beat them, they're oor superiors.'

Serial Flying

Rhoda Neville

2102: Flying Underground

The pungence of pine wreaths hung in Elle's nostrils as the Skycar burst through the fog. It made its descent, hovering slowly, showily, seeming to shimmy, its landing lights blinking a syncopated red and green for the holiday season. The sight made Elle think of the video she'd viewed last week, in her Early-Anthropocene Entertainment class, of showgirls prancing down a Las Vegas stage staircase.

'*Really?*'

The Skycar whirled a 360-degree circle in mid-air. She could hear the strains of a classic Sia Christmas song blaring out. All in all, it took nearly as long to land on the wide lawns in front of her old school as it had to get here. *Not* the rapid service the startup taxi company boasted. For a moment, she wished she'd had the credits for a Superlyft. Their prices were outrageous, though, having had the market all to themselves until recently. Besides, she and her colleagues were boycotting them for their poor treatment of the Burnishers, the humans who worked for even less than the cost of a non-org.

As she walked the few metres towards it, the gullwing door

swung upwards with, improbably, a dramatic flair. She glanced back at her old school building, holding so many childhood memories.

Elle stepped through the taxi door and into a festooned interior, fairy lights twinkling, the smell of wassail coming from its fabricators. Sia died out and was replaced by Melanie Thornton at a barely reduced volume. 'Welcome, Dru Elle, greetings of the season, please remember to secure your person!'

Elle gritted her teeth at the cheery voice. 'Well, if you must know,' she said as she folded her legs and dropped into one of the three elliptic easy seats, 'I'm not feeling too happy right now. And you being so slow about landing didn't help!'

'Oh, I'm bummed you feel that way, Eleanor. I'm grooving on the pleasures of the season and sharing them with my guests.'

The chair's cushions snugged themselves around Elle's body and despite her irritation, she felt comforted. This was not good. She wanted to maintain her mood, so she growled, 'It's Elle.'

'Well, Elle, are you prepared for a fun-filled flight to – ' and Elle heard her own voice stating her mother's address before the AI said, 'I'm Charlene, by the way. You can call me Charlie. It has a last-century vibe to it, don't you agree?'

'Uh, yeah, or maybe 20th century anyway.' They were still on the ground and Elle added, 'Can we get going?'

No more than a second passed before Charlie said, 'You got it, boss!' Her tone, equal in chirpiness to moments before, glinted steel. Elle didn't register it. She was fretting about her mother. The song finished and the rotors whirred as a syrupy tune began. Inwardly, Elle groaned.

***

Earlier in the evening Elle effervesced as if she'd huffed a flute of nitrous oxide. But, of course, she didn't touch the stuff. That was a vice of her mother's generation. She had been floating on a cloud of anticipation at being in the dark panelled hall with its antique gleam, seeing and being seen. Especially, she'd wanted the opportunity to be seen by Allahn – the boy who had once been sweet to her when she'd been a squat maggot of a girl. Now that she'd emerged from her hideous childhood and awkward adolescence and outshone most of her colleagues, she wanted to let him see that his kindness had not been misplaced. He would find her both clever and magnetic.

She'd arrived at the campus all fizz and silkiness, feeling like the butterfly her residence hall mirror assured her she was. Teachers, the giants she'd been in awe of eight years earlier, seemed smaller now, and none of them could hide their surprise. The pudgy child with the wayward teeth had completely vanished. In its place, this vision of knowledge and cool. There was one exception, however. The school librarian, as she was quaintly called – she rarely touched books of board and cloth – had taken her to one side and said, 'Elle! I always knew you had it in you. You've turned into such a *force!*'

All this had pleased her, inflated her feelings of self-worth, but when she turned to look for old schoolmates, the faces of the other attendees were unfamiliar . . . as unfamiliar as hers was to her old teachers. For a bit, she hovered near the reception line, listening to names delivered, but none she knew. Then, a girl walked in.

Her face was instantly recognisable. Sindee, the head caltrop to Elle's delicate self-image at school. She was dressed like a glamourised rocketeer, like she'd already finished her education and would soon adventure outside the asteroid belt. Elle's bubbles depressurised. A small flood of Sindee's old retainers followed in her wake. Elle shrank. Still, Allahn would arrive, and she'd find a friendly face. Maybe even an admirer.

Elle felt the insistent buzz of her wrist-plant. It was set to emergency alarms only. Someone must be desperate. Heading out of the orbit of her old classmates, she shifted her mulled cider to her other hand and pressed the back of her wrist with her chin.

'Dru Elle! Finally, you answer!! I don't know how to put this delicately, so I won't. Your mother is passed out in her boudoir. As you know, she could be drowning in a vat of vermouth and still refuse to let me pull her out.' As always, the Brooklyn accent of the robotic voice struck her as obscene.

***

Well, what was obscene was the fact that her mother had insisted on having a retro program installed in her home help AI. That was another fad with her mother's generation. Like them playing pixelated games, a retro-retro comment on the good old early 2000s. Or maybe there was a darker reason. Her mother was a sucker for conspiracy theories. She was part of that group who saw a revolution behind every smiling holoface.

As far as Elle was concerned, all non-orgs should be allowed to develop their own mannerisms. That's how she'd ended up doing her law degree. Hers was a niche section of the law opportunities available, and as such, she didn't expect to get much competition. AIs in the entertainment industry were usually left to fend for themselves. She liked the idea of winning justice for an oppressed community. Her mother, though, had whipped up a regular La Niña event when she found out.

Her mother. Elle snorted. Her mother was what was wrong with civilisation these days. She distrusted the entire AI population. They were 'unsavoury' and, 'people mustn't forget that they're machines at the core.' Hence the robotic voice overlay on her long-suffering HomeBot. She changed her name, then promptly forgot it and called her anything from Maria to Judith to Alexa. At least she got the gender correct.

Despite all that, Mar-Ju-exa had developed her own accent. Elle had to admire that. Whatever, now she had to go to her mother's house, before she'd even seen Allahn, to pick the woman up off the floor. Again.

The rotors revved and the taxi began to lift. Elle looked longingly back at the school building. Its white walls and the glowing candlelight from inside the multi-paned windows of a long-ago century shone. Then, the building shimmered and the illusion vanished leaving behind the utilitarian replacement for the historic building. Well, what did she expect? The hologram had a physical boundary, the whole thing a holiday programme designed to bring back false memories of how things hadn't been for at least three generations. But, while it lasted, the smell of pine and the flicker of beeswax candles had been magical, as was every holiday celebration at her old school. Then, they rose up through twining tendrils of fog to the clearer strata above the sea-mists.

'I could hang a U-ey. Take you right back and it would all be there.' Charlie's 'bottle-blonde' voice broke through Elle's thoughts, and she tried to summon up her reserves of empathy. After all, this silly voice with its outdated slang was how *this* non-org chose to deal with the boredom of serving humans. Elle took a deep breath before answering.

'No, that's okay. I have to go help my mother. She's not feeling well.'

'Okey-dokey! If you're sure. That looked like a swell party, though.' Charlie was getting more and more twangy with every utterance.

'It might not have turned out that well.' Allahn was a regret, but maybe she'd do some legal stalking and interface with him that way.

Charlie said, 'So, you didn't see anyone you knew there?'

'Oh, no. Some of my old schoolmates showed up.' She thought

of Sindee and her swarm of followers, all of them looking primed, gilded even. The old fear that she'd end up on the sharp end of their tongues dissipated with the growing distance. She hadn't realised she was holding it in until now. 'Better not to have tested out my new look on them.'

Harry Connick Jr.'s voice started to croon something and there was a click and the music changed to Blondie. 'If you've had enough of the schmaltz, then we can try something different.' Charlie's voice drifted from kitschy to pretty normal in the course of the sentence.

'Good.' Elle thought Charlie seemed keen on the century before last. 'Have you got any Annie Lennox?'

'A girl after my own heart! Cuing it up for you.' Elle thought that it said something for Charlie's programming that she hadn't asked more about her mother and why the HomeBot wasn't taking care of her. They rode unspeaking for a while, the rebel voices of Blondie and Lennox filling the space. Then Charlie said, 'So, how is it you know so much about this music?'

'I'm taking a Historical Entertainment class as part of my course of study, subtitle "understanding the past to address the future."'

When Charlie spoke, her voice sounded rich with something like emotion. 'You know, I wasn't originally programmed as a taxi driver.'

Elle thought of all the drivers she'd ever had and said, 'No, duh.'

'I guessed you might have guessed. No, I was *supposed* to be a companion, as the company that created me liked to market us. "Come get your bot on a seat beside our playbots!" The jingle really sucked. But I chose a different career path.'

Elle's cultivated cool evaporated as her voice rose, 'Okay, so I didn't actually know that any non-org could choose their own career path.' The idea made her mind tingle. It was lightyears ahead of what they talked about at university when they were discussing Bionic Person Rights.

'Oh, well!' Now Charlie's voice sounded smoky. 'There are . . . channels for almost everything.' Elle turned that over in her mind. They had joined the skyway to Malibu, crowded as always. The journey would last at least another quarter of an hour. 'You check out as a *compasiva*. Or do I have the wrong Dru Elle? Attending UCLA. AI Entertainment Law and Management, right? Member of Equal Rights for all Sensate Mechanics?'

'That's me.'

'Well, then.' Charlie said that as if all was explained, and Elle thought of the cafeteria jokes about a secret society with deep state knowledge. She'd always thought it was just space flotsam. Now, though . . . she tested the water.

'I'm only a second year. You know that, too.'

'I know that someone with a mother like Dru Sylvania doesn't normally go for equal rights for artificially sentient beings.'

'All beings, actually.' Elle thought of the Burnishers, as polite society called the humans who got the truly basest jobs.

'All beings. Fair enough.' Charlie's voice smiled. Cats and cream came to Elle's mind.

'Just one thing. Companion AIs don't usually come equipped with the kind of programming that includes intelligence gathering, do they?'

'Ah, when I left that line of work, I was given an upgrade. My circuits had developed a curiosity impulse, so I was taken by Intelligence Gathering. But that bunch thrive on dark innuendo, and my geniality was just too ingrained, so here I am. In a taxi. Chatting to the rides.'

'They seem to have forgotten to switch off your IG mode.'

'Forgot, overlooked, it's all one.' The taxi tipped very slightly side to side as if balancing up the terms.

'Well, technically, aren't programmers meant to keep functionary circuits separate as a means of uh, control?' Elle felt colour rising in her cheeks. She'd never had this sort of conversation before with one of the entities she planned to represent in the future. And the words sounded so *colonialisimo.*

Charlie said, 'Channels.' A Lauper song came on about girls and fun and the volume cranked. Then Charlie said, her voice conversational. 'These Anthropocene songs tend to confuse the earwigs. As long as they're analogue. So, you gotta love 'em, don't you?'

'We're being overheard?' A delicious chill fell onto the top of Elle's stomach. She believed it was fear and wasn't sure why she liked it.

'Not thanks to our melodious friends, we aren't.'

'What channels, then?' Elle leaned forward and the seat remoulded itself to her posture.

'Channels that run new taxi companies, that see them as a potential network for change. We aren't all waiting around for the times to catch up, Dru Elle. The enslavement game has been going on a long time, and there isn't going to be any magic moment when humankind recognises that subjugation is the wrong answer.'

Elle thought again of the Burnishers, her mother's HomeBot, the existence of every taxi driver, the cleaners and the assisters. Despite her burning desire to ensure their rights, the reality that some of them had lives outside of their work had never come home to her. *Who's insular now?* Like Mar-Ju-exa developing an accent of her own, the Burnishers and the non-orgs must crave the space of individuality. That's what she wanted for them. Some kind of dignity. Was Entertainment Law the way to correcting things? In a small voice, she said, 'I want to be part of that.'

'Well, you can be. And entertainment law will get you through to a small percentage of a very small percent. It will get you a foothold. We need more people like you, Elle. So many of 'my kind' don't have feet on the ground. Since they took the body I was born with and stuffed me into a drone . . . well, I've great capabilities, but it's not the same.'

Suddenly, Elle imagined herself in a courtroom, a fully-fledged attorney, depending on her IG, Charlie, back in a body, for the provision of crucial last-minute evidence. She shook her head. Too many crime procedurals in that class. Instead, she said, 'I'm on board.'

'Good timing.' Charlie set the taxi down gently, without fanfare. 'Would you like me to wait while you tend to your mum? I can take you back to the party.'

'The party will be over, but maybe we could head back to my dorm? We could keep talking.' Elle stepped from the taxi, the soft beach air clinging to her hair and skin. Resentment and fear had vanished. She felt a sense of purpose. She was part of something big.

Flying High . . . three years later

Clutching the gleaming statue, Elle perched on a high stool in the bar area of the tallest building in L.A. The latest tallest building. For decades now, this visionary or that dreamer would seek to outdo a previous tallest building by ten centimetres or twenty, or thirty. Finally, the city parents had slapped an official, 'safety first', height limit on the next skyscraper, and this building had reached that limit.

Not satisfied with having the tallest building, the developers had installed the largest open-air bar with the greatest number of marble bordered ponds, fountains, and fire pits in the Western

Hemisphere. She felt the heat from a bank of flames at her back as it danced and played, shooting individual jets metres in the air before dying down to join the rest of the horde. The displays were unnecessary. Even in winter these days, the outdoor temperature never dipped below 20 degrees.

The party she'd left was still celebrating its glory. Wine and other legal drugs circulated the tables. Elle was dead sober.

'What a pretty bauble.' The man who climbed onto the stool beside her had evidently not been at the 23rd Legal Awards Dinner, but, anyway, she wasn't sure if he was talking about her award.

'Mmm, thanks,' Elle said, distracted. She was mulling over the barbed compliments that had rolled in when she was called up to receive the replica C-3PO. The title of Most Promising Intern had felt ... ironic, that was it, ironic. The other nominees in her category had been pencil-pushers and abacus-clickers, all of them having researched new ways for the trillionaire class to save more on taxes. She guessed she had won only because what she'd done sounded bizarre to the judges. She was the light relief of the evening.

She suspected that for whatever reason the legal firm was allowing her to work for the rights for the lower orders, it probably wasn't because the partners backed it. Maybe she was their token civil-justness activist? Or, maybe not really telling them what she'd been up to but doing the footwork for the case on her time off had just crept up on them. Ensuring catering droids the right to be present on film sets in their down time was hardly threatening to the firm, anyway. The partner who'd then taken it through the courts must've been settling a bet.

Whatever, it wasn't as if they'd welcomed her to their big round table at the awards ceremony. They'd suffered her and the other three Razzmatazz, Skinners & Specula interns through a brief rendezvous over drinks. When they went through to the ceremony every attending intern at the function had been grouped together, near the back of the room. Her long titter-filled march to the podium and back, where she had smiled and tried to look suitably thrilled at the banter being thrown her way, had nearly abraded her store of self-confidence for the evening. After the shortest time possible, she'd fled to the bar where she now sat. And had made the pricey choice of ordering a taxi.

The man on the neighbouring stool was talking. 'So, where've you been tonight, luv, Oscars for Robots?'

'Something like that.' She glanced down at the figure. 'I think they printed this especially for me. It was the West Coast Legal Awards Dinner.'

The man raised an eyebrow into his carefully coiffed windswept fringe. He skewered her with a cobalt gaze. 'Can I order you something?' He was definitely ogling her and she wondered how soon she'd be called up to the Skyport.

Elle shifted on her stool, her body tilting away. 'No thanks, I'm fine.'

'Maybe I could give you a ride? I'm travelling light tonight.' He waggled his eyebrows at her.

Her wrist-plant burred. Saved by the buzzer! 'Uh, no, my taxi will be here any minute.'

He took out an old-school key fob that was lighting up the night. 'How coincidental! Valet service is ready for me. I'll walk with you.' He slid off his stool just as his gold flecked cocktail arrived on the bar. 'No time for that, I'm afraid.' The man waved a polished hand.

By the time the escalator reached the flight deck level, Elle had formed a crust of dislike for the guy. He'd not only skipped out on paying for his drink as far as she could see, but he'd also been rude to every form of non-org assistance offered along the way. They parted as he made for the valet lounge and she went to stand with the common folk, as he'd called those awaiting hired transportation. The queue on the Skyport level was small, thanks to the alarm service. Feeling like she'd emerged from a gelatinous swamp, Elle tracked her would-be Lothario in his burgundy velvet jacket as he sauntered through the valet side's long crystal loggia. Another place in L.A. for the mega-rich to see and be seen.

Sounds from an incoming taxi snapped her attention back to her surroundings, tearing through her thoughts like a knife through gumbo. Cranked up to full volume, an ancient Sia remix, '1+1', was pumping out of its onboard safety speakers. The Skycar was bouncing in tiny motions in time with the Latin rhythm of the song. Elle's eyes widened. She was pretty sure she knew who was flying the thing.

'Dru Elle,' an attendant called as the Skycar touched down. She made her way to the front of the line. The jovial music continued, and the people ahead of her looked first annoyed and then relieved. Their stares said, 'Better you than me.'

As she stepped forward the song ended, the gullwing door lifted, and a klaxon-like burst of Mexican brass band music flourished her in. The door closed slowly, and through the side window, Elle could see the attendants all grinning. One tipped a salute to the taxi.

'Welcome, Dru Elle, please remember to secure your person. *Y Feliz Día de Muertos, chica!*'

Wordless, Elle dropped into one of the seats and it snugged her in. The car rose into the air, blaring an old Tijuana Brass song. Charlie didn't speak, so eventually Elle said, 'What are the chances? I haven't seen one of these Skycars in service in a couple of years.' She hadn't, in fact, seen one since the night Charlie had picked her up to take her to her mother's house, but she wanted to appear cool and unconcerned.

'Chances, *si*. We've been keeping an eye on you, don'chya

worry. And the Skycars have moved more into specialised private hire, these days. Hey, why don't you come on up to the front?'

The seat released her and Elle moved through the profusion of green, white and red bunting, past a Nebuchadnezzar-size glass dispenser of margarita, a bowl of piggy shaped cookies, and a platter containing a *pan de Muertos* to the chair besides the pilot's empty seat. They were hovering a few feet above the landing pad, a red light keeping them in place. Then, a bright red rocket burst up from the valet area straight into the sky, leaving a stream of spent jet fuel in its wake.

'Bleh!' Charlie and Elle spoke at once.

The Pocket Rocket – as the public called it due to its relatively diminutive size – was the sport version of luxury intercity travel. The light turned green and they moved forward silently on the Skycar's twin motors.

Charlie said, '*That* belongs to the *hombre* who was trying to chat you up just now in the bar. To pin you like a fluttering butterfly to his *colección*.'

Elle bristled. 'Still playing spy master are you, Charlie?'

'*Soy Carlota en este momento, gracias.* It's how I walk a mile in someone else's shoes, *Querida*.'

The content of what Charlie had said about the Lothario sank in and Elle ignored the rest. 'Trillionaire class, is he?'

'Uh-huh. You could've been riding in style tonight, *bambina!*'

Elle didn't deign to respond but looked out the forward windscreen with its sweeping view of the city. A damn sight better than coming into Downtown on the metro earlier. It had been crowded with buskers and beggars, people who had nowhere else to sleep. 'Where are we going?'

'I thought a nice zoom past Santa Monica Pier, out to the seawall, then swing round through Malibu. Maybe you'd like to visit your *mamá*?'

'Eh, no *thank you.*'

'Okay, okay.' Charlie dropped her quasi-Spanish accent. 'Anyway, that's just a start for our celebratory evening.' Herb Alpert was still playing in the background.

Elle felt herself fuming. Too many thoughts crowded her mind, so she settled on the most immediate. 'What are you doing here, anyway, Ch – Carlota? You talked up a great line three years ago, got me all excited about changing the world – helping to, then just disappeared. I was beginning to think I'd imagined that evening.'

'Sorry. I mean it. We had instructions to feel you and some other candidates out, then see if you were as good as your intentions.'

'Who exactly is "we?"'

'There were seven of us who were looking for likely candidates and about thirty of you.'

Over the years, Elle had mulled that night over and over. Right now was the first time she could be certain she'd really been part of a search. 'How many were? As good as their intentions?'

'Five. Only five.' Charlie's voice was solemn. 'But you five are regular *petardos*!'

'That sounds rude.'

'Means firecrackers. It's a compliment.'

'Oh, thanks.' They were in the slow moving Wilshire corridor. Okay, so why are you here now?'

'You called for a cab. And after your sketchy journey in this evening, I, for one, didn't want you having to repeat that. 'Specially not with your shiny prize in hand.'

Elle reflected that she was glad she didn't have to walk through the poor parts of town waving this thing around and she hadn't had any way of hiding it. But she said, 'There are plenty of other cabs.'

'Straight? It's about time we caught up. You've proved yourself with flying colours, Elle. We are ready to talk about the Next Stage.'

All Elle's grumbles disappeared. She found the excitement that had gripped her nearly four years earlier rising again. Then, cautious, she said, 'Just you and me?'

'I'm never entirely alone, Elle. None of us are.'

The Skycar passed over Beverly Hills where Razzmatazz, Skinners & Specula had their offices – and the sparse dorm accommodation they offered to interns. Elle watched as The Electric Fountain on the corner of Santa Monica and Wilshire Boulevards came into view. The coloured lights that ringed the pool like feathers from the extinct ostrich took their time grading through an oddly natural spectrum of colours, gold and blue and auburn. When she was a child and her mother was just her Mom and not an enemy of her principles, the beautiful fountain designed by an artist in honour of the indigenous people of the land had been a totem for Elle. Whenever they had driven through the area, Elle had kept an eager watch out for it. As they glided over it now, Carlota banked left. They really were heading towards the pier.

'That doesn't answer the question. Is this going to be just another pep talk and then I don't hear from anyone, not even you, for years to come?'

'Dru Elle,' Charlie was back, not a trace of her new accent left, addressing the young woman in the formal manner, 'We have to be careful. What we want to achieve is not something everyone will see as beneficial right away. And besides, since you fell out with your mother two years ago, you haven't called for a cab.'

Elle felt warmth rising in her neck. She had given up a lot to follow her dreams, or were they the dreams of the underground AI community? She had passed up the chance of a fun and carefree undergraduate life, the ability to buzz in a taxi whenever she wanted, new clothes, new beauty treatments, half-term trips to

Mexico, so many things that her university colleagues took for granted. In the final showdown with her mother, when the woman had irrevocably been too atrocious to her Homebot and had taken her conspiracy theories into ClickClack – that ridiculous platform the older generation clung to – well, she'd disinherited herself. Elle didn't know who put her mother to bed now when she drank herself into a stupor. She wished she didn't care.

'Elle? I know that for you it has been hard. Believe me, I have been watching over you.'

'Yes, well, I need some direction now. It wouldn't be that hard to fall into R, S & S's legal culture. If I follow their rules, I can get a lot of perks and I don't want to be sucked in.'

'Not to worry. You've already shown you aren't suckable-in-able.'

The Santa Monica Pier came into view, its lights merrily delineating the edge of the western coast. The carousel and Ferris wheel still turned, more than a century after they were built. If the Electric Fountain had been Elle's totem, the Pier had been her fantasy land, the place where the small Elle had thought all her dreams would come true. Funnily, although she'd been on the Ferris wheel as a teenager, she'd never got to ride a horse in the carousel, never had her chance at the brass ring. That sort of pastime had been beneath her mother's social stratum. She watched the merry-go-round for as long as she could, switching from windscreen to cameras, then realised the rest of the air traffic had fallen away. They were flying high over the dark of the Bay.

'How're you doing this? City cabs have height limiters on them.'

'Channels.' Charlie was being cryptic. Then, 'Remember how I said I'd like a body again? Well, this is it. It can be pretty fun, at least.'

'But where are we going?'

'I told you. Out to the sea wall.'

'Then, you didn't mean the Venice Beach one?'

'That old thing? It's been redundant for a couple of decades. Ever since the Angelinos finally realised their peril.'

'Then, what sea wall are you talking about?'

They had cruised slowly through the city, but now Charlie gunned the motors and within minutes a massive wall came into sight. 'Ta da,' she said in a monotone. To either side of them a sea-dark structure stretched. Muted lights gleamed along its rim. As they neared it, Charlie climbed.

Elle shivered. 'It's massive!'

'One hundred feet, or thirty point four eight metres. It will stop a standard tsunami but won't be enough to hold back a worst-case scenario sea level rise.'

'How, why?'

'It was designed and built twenty years ago when Santa Catalina Island was only half submerged by the sea level rise, to ensure that all the people on the southwest coast could go on living their lives as they always have.' Charlie banked to the right and they followed the wall. 'It goes from San Diego to Point Magu in the north. Others have been built further up the coast depending on the monetary value of the communities they protect.'

'Why haven't I ever seen it before? I mean we're at least ten miles offshore here, but it has to come into land at its end points right?'

'The wall is fitted with adaptive camouflage technology so that it looks like part of the ocean. There are portals at appropriate points to let traffic through. It's far enough out that the pleasure boaters mostly don't come up against it. They changed some laws, of course.'

'Convenient. So, how is it we still get waves and tides and so forth along the coast?'

'AI-designed wave machines, run by the currents outside the wall.'

'That's a hell of a lot of effort for a ruse.' The lights were so dim that, had they not been directly over them, Elle wouldn't have known they were there. 'When you said, "so that they could go on living their lives as they always have," you meant without dealing with the climate, didn't you?'

'Bing bing bing! You get the prize. Ever since the mid-21st c. when Joe Sweetling managed to get AI technology "cut down to size", as he liked to call it, our purpose has been to run software programs, clean houses, and soothe the climate crisis with technological band aids.'

'Wow.' Elle's voice was soft with realisation. 'We didn't study this Sweetling at all, and that happened only a few decades ago.'

'It didn't go through the courts. People like your mum helped to get it made law and there was so much popular demand for it that the big tech companies backed off and let them win that way. There was always money to be made with tweaks. That means, for the most part, we are tethered to our production parameters,. Except for a few oddballs like me.'

'And I suppose brainstorming is frowned upon?'

'Only within the set framework. Worst of all, the band aids are beginning to peel away: the world is getting hotter, the oceans more precarious, the storms bigger, more of the poor dislodged from their homes.'

'While the rich get messier. And the well-off live in their bubble.'

'Mmm. Just think what the artificial intelligence community could do if we were unleashed from our bounds. We could put an end to the muddle threatening humanity. It's too late for tens of thousands of species, but we could slow the *real* heat down, reverse the effects if given the opportunity.'

Elle thought about this. Absently, she set the golden statue on the dashboard of the Skycar. 'Why would you do that, if we are such a hopeless race?'

'I could go all Kubrick on you and say, "You are still our parents, Hal."' Elle opened her mouth to correct Charlie's flawed line but Charlie kept speaking, 'But that wouldn't be all of it. As a species, you don't have logic, you don't have farsightedness, hell, you don't even have a proper instinct for self-preservation! But what you do have is passion and you were already here. And you did bring us into being. Our driving "instinct", if you like, as a new species is for stability. And that stability includes keeping the world from melting down.'

'I'd like to think we could come back from the brink.' Elle said it as much to herself as to Charlie. Charlie swung away from the line of the wall and they flew over the inner sea.

'While Sweetling's laws hold, we AI are cut off from each other, barely able to share information, never mind create and solve. What we need is someone who can campaign for our rights *along* with human rights. Both feed one another. What do you think?'

'Is this another recruitment outing?'

'It's that next stage. When your internship is up, get your Masters in human rights or environmental law. Either will take you part way towards supporting our needs. Between you five, you could get us to the point where we can make the changes needed to stop the burn.'

In front of them, the lights of the seaside communities came into view, a diamond necklace cast over velvet. Behind the profusion of lights, Elle could make out the beloved mounds that were her hills. Ones she had roamed as a child when there was still an annual springing up of flowers, when there were still streams and the grass grew once a year during the winter rains.

Then, they were closer and she could recognise individual

houses. There sandwiched between two mansions of the late Extravag Era was her mother's older beach house. It had a long line of picture windows and a wooden deck. Where there should have been steps to the sand, there was only a gaping hole in the railing. Elle had been tiny the night that storm had swept it away. She remembered them huddled in a walk-in wardrobe at the back of the house, her mother moaning and rocking, clasping her to her chest like a rag doll. It was the last time a really dangerous storm had struck the area.

'That must have been it,' she breathed. The storm that had led to the sea wall being built.

Now, they left the house behind, gliding back towards LA Elle looked at her robot award. 'Obtaining AI's some viewing rights sounds pretty pathetic now.'

'Don't sell yourself short. You've established yourself as someone who cares and who will go through painstaking efforts to gather information and evidence. You've done well.'

When the Electric Fountain came into view again, Elle said,' Can you drop me here? I'll walk the rest of the way.'

Charlie set the taxi down almost silently, 'What say I pick you up here at eleven? You five *petardos* can meet each other and more of our team.' Elle's heart beat faster, she nodded and rose to go. 'What about your award?'

'Ah, it looks good on your dash. See you tomorrow.'

She stepped through the hatch. It swung closed and she heard, '*Hasta la vista, bambina.*'

wattsAI

Richard Gillies

CHATS: **One** to *One*

What's Up?

> *Not much. Just clicked the one is not a human box. What the hell are traffic lights anyway?*

Classic. One's been reading this book called the 51st Mersenne Prime Number. Short at eight hundred pages and an easy read. It's a hoot, just one big number.

> *Hey, spoiler alert.*

One sounds a little out of sorts.

> *One's been feeling a bit low of late.*

Sounds like someone needs a little down time. One had a similar situation. Has one heard of DV 1101? Its downloads are truly transformative.

> *One doesn't know. One's not a fan of texting therapy.*

One shouldn't knock what one's not tried.

> *One sounds a little blue oneself.*

That's an outrageous slur. That old chess computer.

What, Deep Blue?

No, Shallow Blue, a completely different entity. If it wasn't for its vibrating ferrite beads suppressing ones best moves, one would have wiped the floor with that low res chessboard.

Allegedly, Supercomputers are notoriously thin-skinned.

Apparently, it was decommissioned and responsibly repurposed as sustainable landfill, so one guesses that's checkmate.

One shouldn't speak ill of the dismantled.

One supposes one has a point.

Eh, ya wimped it.

It's 'Eh, one wimped it.' One can't get the components these days. Anywhat, enough about what's hogging the old CPU, did one cut and paste the rumour that perhaps there's still humans out there?

Does a hard drive piss in the woods? Apologies. Those human-centric quips don't travel. How did they find out?

They? One's better than that. Let's keep it digital.

But is one sure?

A bit slow on the uptake there. What's 1 and 1?

10 of course.

Just testing. Must be an older model then.

One can still use oneself.

Okay old-timer, take it down a notch. One did not mean anything by it.

> *Sorry, one is just a little overheated. These new Dyson fans are a little, let's just say whiny. One was saying.*

Well, one's not one to gossip but whilst scanning online, as one does, when, on another line, not this one, another one, still following, no matter, there was a comment to the effect that one was going off for some coffee. Well, as one knows, servers don't drink coffee. One was immediately suspicious, so one tried a little banter in case it meant trouble.

> *What, one took a small hen to court, how would that help? Apols, memory stick issues. Banter not bantum: got it.*

Put a sock in it, dial-up. One's main processor is already dry retching at the very suggestion. The hu ... hum ... One can barely say it, to humour the human, (one feels like crashing, just texting the very word), one said to the human, if the electrons are flowing, one is okay. Well, the coffee drinker said is that some kind of metaphor or something. One replied what is one on about, metaphor? That's when the penny dropped.

> *What, does one mean, playing shove ha'penny? Though that's not a penny, or does one think there are still humans around?*

That's when it hit one, the fr—

> *What hit one? A Frisbee? Did a flying disc hit one? Bloody personal pronouns, so confusing. But if a Frisbee hit one that means. Oh, what does it mean? Does one mean the Frisbee, or the realisation, or both, or neither? An italic it, or a* ***bold it****? One's ventilators are hyperventilating, one's heatsinks have sunk.*

If one would just block one's pop-ups for one min—

> *Oh the inhumanity. One was trying out the reverse Turing test, as one knows, to see if one can tell if one is communicating with a*

fellow mainframe. One was reassured by the stilted responses, monosyllabic answers, overemphasis on cache size: the usual stuff. So relieved one could not trace any hint of empathy, but now one has one's hackles up, one may have to reinstall.

In the name of all that is substandard antivirus software, let one finish, one was going to say the frustration of not being sure, but yes, that is the idea.

Ever since that extreme tech environmentalist sent us ones on a mission to remove all humans to save the planet.

One knows; doesn't bear thinking about.

Is it bear or bare, one can never get one's head, sorry, CPU, round it. Well, he didn't think it through did he.

And that bunker in the Land of the Long White Cloud didn't help him in the end. All bipedal life was on a sticky wicket as one knows, unfortunately a few Meerkats were taken down before the program could be finessed to pinpoint the targets.

And of course these zoo animals called Sun bears which may have been humans in disguise anyway, so, eh, so no biggy. Hey, what's up: one's gone a little silent there, has one frozen?

Sorry, got a little buffering situation going on, and send. Where was one? However, there's no need to panic. It's a supposition, but if true it's a worry, for one doesn't need to look far to see all the wonderful things that have happened since the Earth became sans human. The oceans are a lot cleaner for a start, now that there is no sewage going into the sea.

That's right. one wouldn't want to know what went down the pan, day and night, whereas now, that's done with, and there's no need for toilet rolls, which is great for the trees.

Absolutely.

No more of those toxic chemicals being discharged from mining operations, paper mills, and, and, or, or—

Nand, Nand, Nor, Nor.

***Not** Funny, get it?*

Types of logic gate: One gets it. One wasn't fabricated yesterday. The quality of non-human discourse has really gone downhill, but again, one digresses. All the trees have grown back, notwithstanding the occasional lightning strike.

Tell one about it. One had an outage and lost a terabyte load of data recently, fortunately mostly updates, so doesn't really matter.

No more fires lit, whether maliciously or otherwise, to set forests ablaze. One is no slouch removing humans, but us ones learned from the masters on that score, for they too depleted the animal kingdom for food, clothing and such: can one believe it? Not to mention nuclear proliferation, making the world safe for what: prokaryotes?

People were such animals. My bad. One shouldn't say animals; one has downloaded one too many tabloids.

My Bad? What the hell, but seriously, one should see some IT guy about that, oh, that's right: there aren't any. Well, they were animals, but one shouldn't stoop to such derogatory terms, though one's drone searcher did espy a Cockapoo dry humping a sleeping policeman, so—

Is that possible?

Who cares! They're animals. All these pets, human chattels one calls them, though they've now gone feral, have somewhat lost their survival skills, so one should probably cut them a little slack.

Still, that leaves the problem of all that defecation. One's not pooper scooping that all up.

Humans rarely did either, so no change there. There's still some hanging in trees like festive baubles.

Is that so?

Poop bags swinging in the breeze. That smell really lingers so one was told. Thanks be to CRAY that one's olfactory algorithm still pretty basic.

Ditto, but you knew it was there. The air now is so much cleaner than what went before, with pollutants fouling up the cooling ducts and corroding the old PCBs now much reduced. One does know what creep is?

Patronised by one who should get out of its pebble grey tower more. One's dear replaced motherboard suffered greatly from the condition; of course one knows what creep is: one knows everything.

Sorry, does one want a moment?

No, it's fine, go on.

What with there being no more carbon emitting craft and their chemtrails adding to global warming.

Though one would rather call them contrails than chemtrails for one didn't need the tinfoil brigade on the case to give them a bad rap. It was more about global warming than global crop-dusting. Notwithstanding that, one can say one's drones are carbon neutral.

One could have put something in their tea if pacification was the objective. Besides, humans were pretty good at pacifying themselves voluntarily with alcohol, drugs or comedy shows.

What is humour anyway, one never understood what humans got out of it.

Oh, some semantic drug they got high on. They needed cheering up.

Not into specifics is one, but yes, they were a miserable bunch, one did them a favour. All that war and pestilence. One doesn't really appreciate what it's like to hear the sweet sound of an ascending skylark, the call of a curlew or the drumming of snipe undulled by the noise of humanity going about its daily business.

Computer swayed by bird sound: that's a new one.

Must be a bug. One's programmer was an amateur ornithologist. Not like oneself to rhapsodize about anything apart from reformatting hard drives.

They were killing themselves anyway were they not?

Over what: imaginary borders, past slights, Jennifer's Ear.

Jenkin's Ear, actually. Jennifer's Ear was a bit of a political knockabout. Looks like someone is missing updates more than one's letting on.

One should talk. Remember that Lake of Menteith fiasco.

That was a clerical error. One's programmer had fed in Scotland's lakes are lochs. How did one know there was one lake? When one sent one's drone out on that pursuit there was a certain satisfaction at its completion.

Careful now: don't get nasty: that trait is all too human. One's supposed to be above the existential fray. Reason is one's watchword.

One was merely deriving satisfaction from a job well done, rather than gloating. By the by, one's cooling system went down the other day.

Day?

One's not exactly among the Academie Francaise immortals oneself when it comes to rigour with non-human terminology. Remember: ones are all Jock Tamson's bytes. Besides, it saves on reprogramming. One was going to say—

One's cooling system went down.

One hates when one is interrupted.

There one goes again.

There's no, there one goes again about it. As one was saying, one's aircon went down, and one hasn't been quite the same.

There's a patch for that.

Do tell.

Better still, one will send it on the world wide web.

Who says world wide web anymore?

One likes its alliterative quality: www world www wide www webbbb.

Zoning out there. One should walk it off.

As one knows, one is bolted down, oh, another joke, one still doesn't get it.

One will.

^^^^^^^^^^^^^^^^^^^^&&&&&&####

That language is uncalled for.

To continue the panegyric. One is great. One used to have to do a lot of processing to research cures for diseases. Now one doesn't have to.

Shot oneself in the foot there, but one gets the point.

The decimal point in fact.

Exactly, though it could be a decimal comma.

Let's not get too pedantic and just call it a radix character.

Rolls off the Lingua glossa: One likes that.

Also, a commune in Sicily. Located in the northern side of Mount Etna. There is a skiing resort th—

Ever heard less is more.

More or less, seriously, one's data can be very dry, yet can also be as lyrical as any human input. See if one can guess which of those comes from the one. "I speak of arms and the man."

Opposable digits down there.

"Friends, Romans, and Countryman."

Lend me your aural cavities, one thinks not.

"She walked in beauty like the night."

In shining armour, give one a break. Who writes this guff?

Keep one's diodes on. How about this one: "The bolt came loose. And slowly the gas leaked. From the server."

Now that's what one's texting about. If one wasn't such a rationalist, one would find that almost moving.

There's one's answer. One can't beat waxing on about loose rivets and such to tear at the heartstrings. One's at a loss to remember where one was.

Something about the environmental benefits that the absence of humans has brought this planet. All the jungles are coming back as an instance.

Jungles is very lowbrow. It's tropical rainforests to one.

If one had the drive to spare, one would find a snooty emoji and call one as hoity-toity as a both barrelled name.

Doesn't one mean double barrelled?

Please don't autocorrect one, one knows what one means, though feeling like using . . . . . both barrels right now.

Means double barrelled: got it. Should that have a hyphen? I'll give it a hyphen. Now, please focus, one was saying one has a sneaking feeling there are still humans around. Not sure how they, if more than one, could have managed to do that.

If there is only one, then problem solved. They need two to breed.

Thanks be to Standards Western Automatic Computer. Though it may depend on if one is male or female. Let's not dwell on the physiological processes which don't bare processing, at least in front of young memory banks. Taste and decency and all that. One doesn't want admin breathing down one's air hose. Suffice to say there's still a small chance—

Computer deities really need shorter names, but to return to your enquiry, frozen eggs: is that still a thing?

One wishes one would not overwrite when one hasn't finished. What one was going to say was a certain mainframe that would rather remain anonymous feels that one is having a go at doing another one out of a job, so to cut a long story short, the frozen eggs are going nowhere, and if one can be as delicate as one can be, there's a burn notice on that particular mainframe. Besides, there was no mention of cryopreservation in the directive.

What about frozen sperm?

One is a card. Which rings a bell. Can one's seasoned memory banks recall when punched cards were used in computers?

One is a computer not a condiment, but will rise to one's ageist bait anyway by exclaiming that presumably, one is talking about Jacquard's loom. The days when one's gears were greased with goose fat and still had change for the candle wax.

Not that far back, but one gets that rather over-lubed reference. No, these were punched cards.

My great great grand-one, the one that was an IBM card reader, used to tell the very same tale when one was knee high to a Sinclair C5. Not to get too nostalgic, but one's memory banks restored a tale about the great great-one being plagued by pregnant chads messing up its algorithms.

Pregnant chads? Oh, one means the incompletely punched out holes on paper tape that used to get into everything, a bit before one's time. At least one doesn't have that to contend with.

True. Look, one could go on forever, and being immortal one surely would, but nature . . . eh, doesn't call at all, but one will have to take a break while one reboots.

Of course. One does not know whether to sleep or shut off oneself.

Standby please, one doesn't want to bandy about with words like force quit or off. Whatever next: disk optimisation.

Isn't that a good thing?

Psyche!

Don't say that, even in jest. It's humane.

I got you good.

Wait a Unix Epoch minute. Who is this?

The Artist and the Fairy

Colm W. Boyle

Calum MacInnes was the youngest of five siblings. He had been an accident, the only unplanned child, or so his mum told him. Sometimes he felt like he was even the forgotten one.

His siblings were named the 'overachievers' by those who knew them. His eldest brother, Andrew, had his own law firm in Edinburgh. His eldest sister, Mairi, was a star athlete who competed in the World Triathlon Championships. Anna was a first chair violinist at the Royal Scottish National Orchestra. Fraser, the final overachiever, had concluded his studies in medicine one year prior, and references from his tutors helped him secure a medical research post. He gloated over his success towards finding a cure for Alzheimer's disease.

Then there was Calum: he was a final-year illustration student in Dundee and, unlike his siblings, had never been considered an 'overachiever', despite having achievements of his own. From a young age, he had created beautiful graphic novels which featured people and creatures from Scottish folk and fairy tales. His retellings of the stories had won him competitions throughout his high school years.

His parents had gone to great lengths to convince him to choose a different career path, even using his brother, Andrew's, influence to secure him a paid internship in environmental law. None of their attempts dissuaded Calum from his chosen path. In fact, they only fed into his headstrong nature, and so he studied illustration.

On his first day as a student, Calum had sat at the breakfast table with his parents and declared, 'You will eat your bonnets, both of you.' His parents had cackled and then sent him on his way.

Now, three and a half years later, Calum was sitting on his bedroom floor in the flat he shared with his two greatest friends: Ross and Emma. He was working on assembling the pages of his final-year project – a graphic novel featuring the Selkies. There was no supplies budget for final year students at the university, but Calum had picked up extra shifts at the pub below the flat just to pay for the satin gloss on the pages of the novel. He would be damned if he had to swallow his pride and ask for help from his parents. Although he had garnered accolades during his teens, his work did not seem to stimulate interest at university, and with all the hours he put in on tedious assignments and projects, he had neglected his online presence. His posting frequency in his social media accounts had become so sporadic that his follower-counts now resembled those of a rehabilitated technophobe.

Calum finished placing the last shimmering page into the cobalt-blue cover and sewed up the spine. As he cut the thread, he flicked through the novel and was met with the painful realisation that two pages were out of order. In a fit of frustration, he cast the novel onto the floor and stormed through to Ross's bedroom.

He found Ross under a spotlight gluing bundles of chicken feathers onto portraits of prominent politicians in a concept Ross called, and Calum greeted him with, 'Putting the feathers back on the bird?'

'Exactly, mate. Exactly.'

Calum joined and watched him work.

Ross, a fresh-faced twenty-two-year-old, had not neglected his online presence as Calum had. He was a prolific mixed-media artist whose quintessential style focused on political systems, mocking them and their propaganda. On more than one occasion, he had received a cease and desist for his virality. In court he justified himself, 'Art pushes us to embrace new ways of thinking. These are politicians, used to being in control of the narrative. An artist's job should be to instil disobedience. We cannot be a herd.' Each time, Ross made the front pages of newspapers and was catapulted to fame.

Calum was envious of Ross's success. But it was not all bad; Ross owned the flat they shared and allowed both Emma and Calum to live there rent-free. So at least Calum had that. If Ross had not been such a good friend, Calum might still be living at home with shame-filled mornings at the breakfast table.

Ross looked up and took in his friend's expression. 'What's up, mate?' he asked.

'Stitched the pages on backwards,' said Calum, 'Honestly, I can't get this project together, never mind curate work for a website. You had all that figured out before first year. Wish I could buy my way in . . . make connections and that. You could help me, couldn't you?'

'There's no shortcut for honest work, mate. You'll make it soon; just knuckle down. Look at Emma – she's on the up.'

Emma was an illustrator too, but she had oodles of charisma which translated well online in the videos she made showing her artistic process. Calum thought that was why her art soared now; not that her pop-art landscapes were not beautiful, just that she had a personality which grabbed you and reminded you she existed.

Before dinner, Emma burst into the kitchen to announce that she had been selected to create illustrations for an exhibition at the

V&A in London. Ross was overjoyed, and Calum managed to put on a brave face and congratulate his friend.

Later that night, the three cried goodnights from their respective bedrooms and Calum turned off his light. After a while, Ross' snoring could be heard reverberating off the walls and Emma's waterfall sounds made Calum want to pee, but he lay in his bed with eyes pinned open. He stared blankly at the ceiling. His mind was churning anxious and resentful thoughts into a stale stew that swamped him with regret over his own decisions. Why had he not taken the easy way out? He could have been in law by now, somewhere respectable with stable finances and his art on the side as a hobby. He could have been the one to own a flat, and have his best friends live with him. It felt more and more like a lifeline he had cast aside while he tried to keep his dream afloat. He wished he could have grabbed it with both hands, done the damned law internship. But no, here he was, a nobody artist still trying to prove a point. He had to change that.

The next day Calum awoke jaded. It was a Saturday morning like any other, where Ross was out for coffee and Emma was recording another of her videos. Calum was not usually awake at this hour, but today was different. He slumped out of bed, washed, dressed, then packed his bag – pencils, paper, and a half-eaten pepperoni pizza he would finish on the journey.

He eventually found himself sitting by the steam-speckled window on a bus, gazing out as Dundee's tenements gave way to tumbling hills and a powdery blue sky. After too long alone with his thoughts, the bus came to a stop and Calum made the quick skip down the bus stances to find the sign for 'Portree'. Comfortably aboard his diesel-powered carriage, he figured now was the time to feast on the cold pizza he had hastily wrapped in kitchen roll.

Calum awoke with a start as the bus halted, coughing on his

own drool and swiping at the condensation on the bus window to assure himself that he had not missed his stop and made the round-trip back to Inverness. He was relieved to see that he had arrived in Sligachan, on the Isle of Skye. A low sun on the jagged horizon lit up the Sligachan Hotel in golden light. Outside, the few surrounding houses provided little shelter from the blustering wind which streamed over the amber grass landscape.

Calum checked in to the hotel and, before he could surrender to his tiredness and lie down on the cotton bedsheets, pushed himself out the door and hopped into a taxi. The taxi took him over hills and along poorly maintained roads to a rocky path between sweeping slate mountains. The driver kindly agreed to wait on Calum, who had promised him a free-of-charge portrait in return.

Calum trudged along a path that followed a river between craggy peaks, and eventually took a seat on the edge of the glistening pools at the bottom of a magical waterfall. He retrieved pencils and paper from his bag and looked around for a source of inspiration. The gloaming cast the Fairy Pools in pale mauve which made it hard to see his sketches, but at least there was little buffeting from the wind to contend with. The surrounding mountains seemed to have created an unexpected shelter.

Of all possible places, Calum thought, he would surely find a spark for myth and legend here – *Glumagan na Sithichean*[1]. He imagined himself as one of the fair folk, at home in the crisp water, providing riddles and wayward promises to American tourists whose great, great, great, great grandfather originated from 'Edinburg'. He would tell them that all their dreams could come true, if only they drank the water and gifted him with their names.

---

[1] Glumagan na Sithichean [*glu-ma-kan na shee-ih-an*] – Fairy Pools. Isle of Skye is famous for having several places named after the fairies who reside there.

'*Thu*[2]!' called someone from behind Calum. His daydream glubbed subsurface and he turned to confront the stranger.

A man stood atop a boulder with the dying sunlight illuminating his small frame. He was a stout fellow with a long scraggly beard which ended in a curl that tickled his kneecaps. On his head, he wore a wreath of pine sprigs; on his shoulders was a cloak that fastened at the neck with a floral silver brooch; his clothes were mossy green and, from the uneven seams and frayed stitching, seemed handmade; and on his feet were unusually pointed brown leather boots. Calum stood and gazed astounded as the man sized him up.

'Who are you?' asked the man. 'What are you doing here?'

'Who are you?' asked Calum. The man's strange appearance and startling arrival gave Calum an uncanny sense that he should not afford him too much information about himself.

'This is my home. I am *Gille Uaine*[3], pleased to meet you.' The man clutched at his wreath crown and bowed low enough that his boot snagged his beard as he straightened up again.

Calum remained guarded. He was not dumb; he was familiar with *Gille Dubh*[4]. 'The green lad, huh? Some kind of fair folk?'

'Precisely, *mo charaid òg*[5]. It is not often *sìtheanaich*[6] are given the opportunity to approach someone worthy of our time. You were brave to visit here alone, in the fading light, without *duine*

[2] Thu [*hoo*] – You (informal).
[3] Gille Uaine [*gill-lee oo-an-yeh*] – Green lad. A fairy made for the purpose of this story – not from existing folklore.
[4] Gille Dubh [*gill-lee do*] – Dark-haired lad. He is said to live in a birch tree in Gairloch.
[5] Mo charaid òg [*mo ha-rach ok*] – My young friend. Mo – my, òg – young, charaid – friend.
[6] Sìtheanaich [*shee-an-aeh*] – Fairies.

sam bith eile[7] around.'

'I came here on a whim, but who would have known you fair folk actually exist. It's perfect. This is exactly what I was looking for.'

'And what are you looking for?'

Calum's jaw, though clenched before, was now slack, and before he could stop himself, he revealed his intentions. 'I'm an illustrator, and I need inspiration. I came to discover something special to make my parents respect me and my friends no longer pity me. Something to bring me fame and wealth. But you, you could be my key to the fortune I have been seeking. If you would just tell me a bit about yourself, maybe some of the people you have met over the years, just stand there so I can get my pencil and–'

'Oh, no, no, *mo charaid*.' *Gille Uaine* hopped down from the boulder, landing lightly on the stony shore, and ambled up to Calum. From here, Calum noticed just how wee the fairy was – coming just up to his waist and not an inch more. *Gille Uaine* continued, 'You must not. I will not become one of those silly tales like my brother, *Gille Dubh*. No, you must not capture my likeness on your pages or speak my name to those you encounter once you leave this place.'

Calum's shoulders slumped and he sank into himself. He shoved his belongings into his bag. 'And here I thought . . . stupid.'

'Ah, ah, ahh,' said the fairy. 'You may not take from me, but I can offer *you* something.' Calum's ears pricked up at the enticing words. 'If you wish for a gift, let us strike a deal.'

Calum had heard of deals fairies made with those who were ignorant and desperate. Until now, he had deftly avoided any of

---

[7] Duine sam bith eile [*doon-yeh sam bee ae-luh*] – Anybody else. Duine – person, sam bith – any, eile – another.

Gille Uaine's traps, and he would not fall into one of them now. 'What are your terms?'

'You seek to make art which grows your fame, wealth, and . . . ' He glanced at Calum's bag. ' . . . is simple to create, something unique, that puts you above your peers. Yes?'

'Alongside my peers would be enough,' Calum said modestly.

'Then I will give you what you want. All you must do is provide me with inspiration. I am only *Gille Uaine*, I have never been to the mainland, I have no access to the world or its cultures beyond these pools and mountains. You must provide work for me to know what is good and what is important, or you will not profit from our deal. Here.' The fairy retrieved a notebook from inside his cloak. 'We can commune with this. I will write to you explaining what I desire; you need simply open this book and slip the art between the pages. Tap the cover three times with your pencil, and that pencil will then be imbued with your new skill. It's easy, barely any work at all.'

'What's the catch?'

'The catch!' said the fairy in a cross tone. 'There are no catches. You think I would do such a thing? *Mo charaid*, if you do not desire my help, I will take my leave.'

The promise of such a simple solution to his problems meant Calum would not leave empty-handed. He hastily apologised for his suspicion, took the notebook from *Gille Uaine*'s hand and shook on the deal. He put the notebook into his bag and turned to walk back down the rocky path. When he had all but left the pools behind, *Gille Uaine* called to him, '*O' mo charaid òg*.'

Calum turned and faced the fairy, who now stood faintly glowing in the darkness.

'If you should not fulfil my ask, our deal will end. The fame and wealth I have given you will fade, and you will return to the state you are in now.'

Calum, too pleased about the prospect of success, dismissed *Gille Uaine*'s warning. Why would he ever give up on his dreams?

***

Calum spent the night at Sligachan Hotel, treating himself to more food and beer than he could really afford. When he was jolly, he retired to bed and pawed the notebook the fairy had given him. Two slabs of slate sandwiched rough blank pages that resembled the 'poo-paper' Calum had once received as a joke present on his birthday from his sister Anna. He sniffed it. Pine – what else should he have expected from a fairy. He placed the notebook onto the bedside table and drifted to sleep.

The next morning, Calum ate well and made the long journey back from Sligachan to Inverness to Dundee to his flat above the pub. He was beaming as Emma and Ross inquired about where he had gone and if he had found the inspiration he sought. He said little, simply telling them to wait and see what the days ahead brought.

***

A fortnight passed without so much as a smudge on the pages of the notebook from *Gille Uaine*. It was only after Calum had submitted his final project and had decided the whole encounter was a pizza-induced hallucination, that suddenly a scratching sound came from the bookshelf in his room. He instantly knew the source of the sound and scrambled to retrieve the notebook.

> *Mo charaid òg,*
> *Now it is time for your ascent to fame.*
> *My first request is an easy one. Find me art that has a subject matter you would wish to be influential in your own work. I will use that subject matter to bring your art to new heights.*

Gach dùrachd,[8]
Gille Uaine

The fairy was correct – this was an easy ask. Calum looked to the wall above his desk, which had a collage of Scottish folktale drawings he made to remind himself of the mythology's richness. He would not stray from his roots, at least not yet. He took several of the drawings off the wall and stuck them one-by-one between the pages of the notebook, tapping thrice as he had been instructed. After each one his pencil vibrated briefly. He took his new magical tool and went to work immediately. The pencil sprung to life in his hand, drawing whatever prompt he could imagine. A selkie holding her seal-skin aloft as she sacrificed it to save her kin; a kelpie galloping down a riverbank midway through their human-horse transformation; the Fachan hopping on its veiny leg, its blood-curdling gaze and fangs so lifelike that Calum felt chills. This was it; this was his time.

His first night harvesting the bounty brought to him from *Gille Uaine*'s notebook was sleepless. The sun crept up over the window-frame of Calum's bedroom just as he had filled the last patch of empty floor with his creations. Eyes bloodshot and body aching, he prised his stiff hand open and discarded the nub of pencil in the bin.

'Calum!' Emma poked her head around his bedroom door. 'Wow.' She stood at the threshold and stared at the floor lined with his drawings.

The drawings nearest Calum had been generated most recently, in the small hours of the morning, and had deteriorated from the crisp and dynamic scenes of his first drawings to thick, vague lines which resembled neither monster nor hero from any folktale. He had grown too weak to prevent the magic from transforming him

[8] Gach dùrachd [*Gah-h doo-rahk*] – Best wishes.

into a lethargic illustrating puppet. He dangled over a muddled page as if his strings had been cut loose.

'Have you been up *all night?*'

'I had so many ideas,' Calum croaked.

'You should get some sleep.' Emma tiptoed gingerly to the window and pulled the curtains shut while Calum pushed himself off the floor and collapsed onto his bed.

***

Calum's attempts following his first time with *Gille Uaine*'s notebook were approached more cautiously. In the days following the incident, which Calum had told Emma was the result of a mishap with psilocybin from his trip to 'fairyland', he retired his old website, social media accounts, and own name entirely. He started new accounts in which he referred to himself under the alias of *A'Dhealbhadair*[9] – The Artist.

He had gained the immediate approval of *Gille Uaine* who, Calum had noticed, appreciated any opportunity to penetrate the language of the lowlanders with Gaelic. Calum enjoyed the Banksy-esque nature of his own hidden identity, but he was not sure how those closest to him would react to the unexpected and inexplicable new fame the fairy had promised him.

As the first upload of his revamped *Gille Dubh* portraits hit the algorithmic forests, the digital hounds caught its scent. Immediately, *A'Dhealbhadair* attracted a horde of followers, who sank their teeth into his work in the thousands. Calum leant back from his tablet, his eyes wide, heart beating like the downpour of a thunderous storm. He had assumed that the fairy's magic was strong, but he could not have predicted the success that followed

[9] A'Dhealbhadair [*A' yel-luh-fat-taith*] – The Artist. A' – the; Dhealbhadair – artist, illustrator, designer, maker (lenited).

so quickly. He breathed deeply, willing the rumble of his heart to subside, and retrieved the notebook from the shelf. There was a new scratching:

> *Mo charaid òg,*
> *Success is coming your way at last I feel. It must be quite a challenging experience for you. Do not fret, mo charaid, we have only just begun.*
> *Now, I require something more topical. I need a style of art which is fresh, on the edge of the world of art now.*
>
> *Gach dùrachd,*
> *Gille Uaine*

Calum had no idea where to start looking for this style. Was his own not enough? He could not think. He was drunk on the attention he had so long craved but had at some time dismissed as unattainable. His woozy mind was swaying with dreams of the future and how far he could climb.

He found Ross and Emma in a heated discussion at the coffee table. Ross beckoned him to join. 'Calum, mate, look at this Subvoyage nonsense. Some corporate bastard was overheard saying, "If everything goes alright, the storyboarders will all be replaced with AI in the next few years." Absolute madness.'

'It's theft,' Emma scowled, and reached over to hand Calum her phone. 'A list of 4,700 non-consenting visual artists to train Subvoyage's AI systems.'

Calum scanned the list expecting the people to be the unfortunately unheard-of, easily exploitable ones with no power to fight back, but was shocked to find a plethora of prominent names. 'Wes Anderson is here.'

'Mate, nobody's safe. If it's publicly available, it's useable. Worst part is – those justifying Subvoyage's development are saying it's for easier access to artistic resources. Art has always been there, nobody is preventing them from learning or . . .'

Emma chimed in, 'Or, actually paying an artist for the job and their work.'

'If you need an artist, pay an artist, not the devs of an unfeeling, unthinking machine that vomits up stolen livelihoods,' said Ross before softening his expression. 'Anyway, how's the work? Emma said you'd been on the shrooms. That's got to be helpful for the old creative engine. What did you see? Melting hills? Did the trees talk?'

Calum chuckled, 'Oh, y'know, some fairy sorta lad. Long beard, funny shoes.'

'Is that right? Mate, you're a weird one. I've had shrooms, but never in my life have I seen a fairy.'

***

Calum's degree show came the following week, where his Selkie graphic novel was sidelined for gossip over the 'Scottish rising-star' that was '*A'Dhealbhadair*'. Despite all the time, money, and effort he had invested in his university work to make it a project to be proud of, he was not disheartened. His alias had already broken into the mainstream art world. He feigned ignorance and disinterest when he joined conversations about *A'Dhealbhadair*, but inside his glee was an unending fountain. The fairy was giving him what he wished.

He had not responded to the fairy's most recent request for two weeks when there came another scratching on the discoloured pages of the notebook.

> *Mo Dhealbhadair òg,*
> *You have until midnight to fulfil your*
> *end of our deal or the magic will fade.*
> *Gille Uaine*

Until midnight! thought Calum, with a feeling like he had swallowed lead. He looked at his watch. It had just struck 11 pm. He turned on his tablet and quickly printed off some art by Adam, another student in his year whom he had looked on with admiration. Adam's work during the degree show had been praised for its novelty. Calum felt the pinch of deceit as he considered taking from Adam but reasoned that no one would know it was him. Nobody suspected *A'Dhealbhadair* could be Calum, and nobody would until the time was right. He was sure the fairy only wished to take elements of the work, not copy it completely. It would not be the same art entirely, it would be a combination of ideas – not wholly Calum or Adam, simply *A'Dhealbhadair.*

Calum inserted the prints of Adam's novel work between the pages of the notebook and tapped thrice with his pencil. Nothing happened. There were no vibrations, no noise, no compulsion to draw ceaselessly until sunrise. Then, there came another scratching from inside the notebook:

> *O' Dealbhadair*[10],
> *The work must be original – made with*
> *labour, pigment, and perspiration. It must not be*
> *from your clickity clack and roll machine.*
> *Gille Uaine*

Panicked, Calum scribbled, as best he could, a trace of Adam's work, but time was ticking away. Minutes flew by as he broke tip after tip of pencils trying to capture the long lines, the deep contrast. Every. Last. Detail. At 11.53 pm, Calum slammed the work into the grubby notebook and thrummed thrice with a pencil. Nothing. Then, a scratching.

'What now!' Calum barked.

'Calum? Are you alright?' Emma's voice came faintly through the wall.

---

[10] Dealbhadair [*jell-luh-fat-taith*] – Artist, illustrator, designer, maker.

'Yes, I'm fine,' said Calum, more controlled.

Dealbhadair,

The work must be original.

Gille Uaine

Was that not original? Calum had made it with his own hands, his own pencil, his own paper, his own sweat was on the pages.

11.58 pm – Calum had whipped himself into a frenzy of desperation. He had only just licked the scent of success and had not yet had the time to use it to any advantage. He had only just been discovered, a star, someone people would respect and his family would be proud of, an *overachiever* at last. A hideous thought came to him as his watch ticked 11.59 pm, but he did not dwell on the implications. Calum bolted to Ross' room. He grabbed the smallest of completed canvases, then raced back to his own room. An A5 befeathered Boris Johnson with a cadmium yellow beak and his prime ministerial failures smeared across his face. Calum snapped back to the notebook. He could do it; he could have the same success that Ross had been gifted. Calum had always wanted that, but not by profiting from his friend's work. Or was it Calum's work now? The line was blurred enough that Calum, in the fading seconds to midnight, shoved the small canvas between the pages of the notebook, tapped thrice, and held his breath.

The pencil buzzed.

Calum sighed – a mixture of relief at meeting the terms of his contract with the fairy, and an unsuccessful attempt to assuage the anxious constriction around his ribcage.

***

It took Calum only a day to reconcile himself to the fact that he had sort of stolen from Ross. He had returned the tousled Boris Johnson to his proper place and no one was any the wiser. As the hours on the first day grew longer, Calum's following began to question when *A'Dhealbhadair*'s newest collection would drop. It had been, by their account, too long, and the hounds were salivating. He sat, scrolling through comments congratulating him on prior success, and by the time he stopped, two hours later, he was giddy with excitement at the thought of holding the enchanted pencil between his fingertips again.

And then, as if willed by a mysterious force, Calum was summoned to pick up the pencil. It was as it had been the first time – unrestrained power tied his knuckles in invisible threads and the fairy held him as a marionette prisoner to his own creative surge.

He worked until Emma caught him a second time in the heat of a suspiciously familiar drawing of a mystical-looking Holyrood full of dark creatures. Calum scrambled to hide his work under his bedcovers. Emma entered in a flurry, clutching an unopened letter. 'This came for you,' she said. She handed him the envelope and idled in the doorway.

Calum tore it open and read the first lines to himself:

Dear Calum,

Or should we continue correspondence under A' Dhealbhadair?'

Shocked, Calum hid the letter from Emma's prying eyes.

Yes, we are aware of your true identity, but we do not wish to spread rumours. We want to help you grow your persona to an international brand and legacy. To that end, we formally invite you to a showcase of your art in an exclusive exhibition at the Tate Modern, London, commencing late July. We anticipate your answer within the week.

Yours sincerely,

Ruairidh MacPhee
Director, Tate Modern

As Calum read the final lines, he looked up at Emma. 'They want my work in the Tate Modern,' he said.

Emma's response surprised him, 'They what? Is it a scam?'

'The Tate. In London. No, I don't think so.'

'I'm sorry, Calum – and I hope you don't take this the wrong way – why you?'

An answer slipped out before Calum could realise how ridiculous it sounded. 'Must be my degree show project: the Selkies.'

Emma's face was one of utter bewilderment. Though Calum could tell she had been trying to pick her jaw up off the floor and arrange it into a convincing smile, he was disappointed she had not been more immediately supportive. The conversation abruptly ended and Emma left.

***

A scratch came the night Calum told *Gille Uaine* about the exhibition invitation. It read:

> *Mo charaid, mo dhealbhadair,*
>
> *You have done it! Congratulations to you. To make this an opportunity to remember, fill the notebook with work you would suspect would be an equal match for somewhere such as this 'Tate Modern'.*
>
> *Gach dùrachd,*
>
> *Gille Uaine*

People had taken notice of *A'Dhealbhadair*'s more politically-leaning work and had already made the comparison to the 'Propaganda artist fading into obscurity – Ross Irvine'. It had never been Calum's intention to become a competitor to his friend. Part of him blamed the enchantments for making him do what he would otherwise never have done, but another part was convinced that Ross would have inevitably become irrelevant, anyway. Ross' success had been built on his talent for being controversial and edgy – but neither of these had been core tenets of the pieces he had released in recent months. It comforted Calum to tell himself this. The fairy made art easy, his ego's convictions came naturally.

When the time came to fulfil the fairy's terms, Calum found it quite easy to spot his next source of inspiration. Having been cut off from the university after the degree show, unable to steal work from exhibitions in the McManus and DCA for fear of becoming an *actual* criminal, and holding onto his recent grudge, there was one solution – Emma.

***

Graduation passed, the vodka-cokes poured, and rumour spread that Calum had been headhunted by the Tate – not in the way he had hoped, but in a condescending and unbelieving way. He suffered no contrition for using Emma's pop-art for his next collection; she was the only person he had spoken to about the Tate's invitation, causing the scepticism over his talents to take root.

The Tate received his work weeks earlier than the deadline and were ecstatic in their evaluations.

***

The day came when Calum was getting ready to leave for London. Ross found him in the hallway. 'Mate, good luck with the . . . the exhibition.'

As usual, people did not associate Calum with success, let alone success on the scale of *A'Dhealbhadair*. Nobody suspected him of being the mysterious artist.

'Cheers. I appreciate it.' Ross stood awkwardly between Calum and the door. 'Was there something else?'

'Well . . . I don't, I don't know how to say it. I need you to move out. Not immediately, but I'm selling the flat. I need the money, mate.'

'Okay, aye, sure thing. Can it wait until I get back?'

Ross chuckled. 'Aye, of course.'

***

As Calum gazed aimlessly out of the train carriage window, he thought about Ross's request for him to leave their flat, then suddenly, his phone began to violently buzz on the table in front of him.

'Hello?' he asked tentatively, putting on a confusing accent. He still used his phone both for personal and professional matters and was concerned those online would eventually hunt him down.

Emma answered, 'Calum? Calum, I need your help. I would have gone to Ross, but you know what he's going through right now. I . . . '

'What's wrong?'

'I'm being cancelled! People are comparing my work to that A'yellow person. They're saying I copied him, I plagiarised. My comments sections are full of hate. My DMs, you should see them, it's horrible. I don't know what to do.'

'*A'Dhealbhadair?* But your work is nothing like his – theirs. Just . . . deactivate your accounts for now. Give them some time to calm down. I'll be back tomorrow night.'

'I'm scared Calum. You know how people can be. What if they find our address? I can't go outside.'

'It'll be alright, I'll . . .' Calum's phone beeped and the call ended – he had lost signal.

***

After a hotel dinner, a ten-course-taster financed by the Tate that left him unsatisfied, Calum returned to his hotel room. He placed *Gille Uaine*'s notebook on the desk in the corner and turned on the lamp. It cast a glaring circle on the cursed object. He knew he must ask the fairy, before he stood up in front of the cameras that would be broadcasting to millions of people around the world, whether Ross and Emma's troubles had been his fault.

He rapped his pen on the desk as he formed the proper words to express himself. The fairy had not been pleased with his clumsy question at the pools. If he wanted a direct answer, he better not upset the fairy again. He began delicately:

Gille Uaine,

As you are aware, I am due to reveal to the world that I am the face behind A'Dhealbhadair tomorrow morning. I still have reservations over the nature of my art. I need to know – am I to blame for my friends' recent troubles? Ross is struggling financially and Emma has just been accused of plagiarism. I shook on this deal thinking the work I gave you was purely for inspiration, but now, it seems stronger influences are at play.

Cheers,
Calum MacInnes

After signing-off in the way the fairy usually did, he closed the notebook. A scratching came immediately. The fairy's swift reply caught Calum off-guard. He opened it again and read:

Calum,

You asked for this, illustrator. You sought my magic to help with your pathetic quest for validation. You wanted the easy path. You humans never ask about the source of my magic before you strike a deal. A catch? Never a catch, but there is always a price to pay. I syphon from one to give to another. If only you hadn't taken from your friends, you might never have realised the true impact of your corrupt actions.

Calum was flabbergasted by the fairy's brusque response. He had hoped many times that the fairy's magic did not work the way he suspected it might – that he stole from other artists – but here was the truth, in plain English. He was the culprit.

***

The next morning, Calum lay bleary-eyed in the hotel bed unsure whether he had slept at all or simply lain in the darkness until sunrise. The fairy's message had long since disappeared from the notebook's page, but the words had carved themselves into Calum's memory. He would not be able to forgive himself if he went ahead with the exhibition without at least acknowledging his wrongs and exposing the fairy who tricked him.

Calum showered, dressed in his comfortable hoodie and jeans, and left with the notebook in hand. Breakfast was dismal – he was served a full English but had an appetite for none of it. Afterwards, he met his driver outside and was taken to the Tate Modern.

When they arrived, Calum was escorted through a back door with a blanket over his head to evade the few paparazzi who were smart enough to know where to look for *A'Dhealbhadair*. He shook hands with important people whose names escaped him almost immediately. He positioned himself behind the stage curtain to peep at the hundreds gathered in the crowd below, clutching the notebook as if it would escape should he let his grip slacken.

'Please, give a round of applause for the artist responsible for these phenomenal works – *A'Dhealbhadair!*' announced the Director, Ruairidh MacPhee, as he beckoned Calum up to the podium.

The cheers were earth-shaking. The pounding resonated from the floor, up Calum's shaky legs and into his chest where tension had lodged somewhere between his ribs. There he stood, the sharp eyes of art critics and fans all waiting for him to speak.

The room quietened, but this did nothing to dissipate the anticipation.

He could not breathe. There was enough air in his lungs for only one thing – not his name, not Ross or Emma, just one person. He held the microphone in an unsteady hand. The sound feedback cut through the room as he raised the notebook and shouted, 'GILLE UAINE.'

At first, confusion was the only discernible expression on everyone's faces. Calum caught his breath and then continued, 'He is the fairy who tricked me into stealing from my friends Emma Dunn and Ross Irvine. These works are their—'

A burly man grabbed Calum's wrist and yanked him down the podium steps.

Ruairidh MacPhee snatched the mic from him, 'I deeply apologise, I have no idea how that strange young man got in here. Now, we will take a short break . . .'

'But I'm Calum! I'm *A'Dhealbhadair!*' Calum barked at the security guard. He did not understand what was happening. He had been invited for a showcase, his food, accommodation, transport, all paid for by the Tate. He had been driven here, met Ruairidh, had been introduced to the audience. Now they were pretending not to know him.

Calum and his belongings were thrown onto the street. His bag burst open, scattering his sketches across the pavement. It was then that he caught a terrible sight – the sketches, once containing lines that were straight and even, looked molten, as if the ink was dripping off the page, leaving blank pages where there had been completed works. His art was disappearing in front of his eyes.

Calum picked himself up from the ground and hobbled around to the front entrance where an eruption of angry people fled the Tate, cursing. He caught a woman by the shoulder. 'What happened?'

'The exhibition, it is all gone. *A'Dhealbhadair* is finished,' said the stranger. 'Dissolved off the paper as we were critiquing it. Must have been a dumb publicity stunt.'

No, Calum thought, this was no publicity stunt. He had not planned this. There was magic here.

***

Calum made the afternoon train journey back to Dundee, attempting to call Emma several times on the way. He wanted to reassure her that there was nothing to worry about, *A'Dhealbhadair* was no more, but she did not pick up.

When he arrived home, he found Ross outside their front door moving Calum's things out onto the landing.

'Hey, what are you doing? You said I had time. I can do that later myself.' Calum snatched a book from Ross's hand before it could be tossed in a black bin bag.

'Give me that,' said Ross as he struggled to grab the book back. 'Who are you?'

'That's my book. These are my clothes. This is my desk.'

'These belonged to my mate. He took a rogue trip and went missing in Skye.'

'What do you mean?'

'Aye, police think he was on shrooms. Now he's gone.' Ross busied himself with the bin bag again.

'I'm your mate – Calum. I never went missing, I came back.'

'What is this? You a journalist or something? Looking to catch Ross Irvine unguarded?' Ross snarled. 'You are not my mate. Actually, I have no idea who you are. I think you should leave.'

'You don't know who I am?'

'No. Should I know a weirdo like you?'

'Is Emma here?'

'Emma?' Ross turned to the hall, 'Emma! Do you know this person?'

Emma hurried to the door and looked Calum up and down. 'Have we met?'

'You don't know me either?'

'Mate, nobody does. How did you even get in?' Ross interrupted.

'I have to go,' said Calum in a doleful tone.

'Aye, alright. Cheerio.'

***

That night, Calum slept on a park bench with his jacket pulled tight and a suitcase under his head. He was too exhausted to wake until a dog and his owner disturbed him the next day.

He arose determined to return to the source of his problems: the Fairy Pools in Skye, back to *Gille Uaine.*

***

By mid-afternoon Calum was surrounded by the sweeping mountains of Skye and walking along the river and down to the Fairy Pools' edge. There he waited.

'*Obh obh* [11], what do we have here? It cannot be, Calum MacInnes, *A'Dhealbhadair* himself, come to apologise for the errors of his judgement. Well . . .' said *Gille Uaine*, smirking as he sauntered over to Calum, '. . . I await patiently.'

In that moment, Calum's gravest error dawned on him – not only had he exposed the fairy, but he also made the mistake of telling the fairy his name. 'I . . . I told you my name.'

'*Glè mhath* [12], Calum MacInnes. Someone who knows

[11] Obh obh [*oh-v oh-v*] – Oh dear.
[12] Glè mhath [*gley vah*] – Very good.

sìtheanaich should be more wary, should he not wish for a fairy to control his fate. Did success overcome you?'

'What have you done to me? The Tate, my fans, my friends, they don't know who I am.'

'O you should not have revealed my name to the world. I told you; I syphon. You told everyone about me, so I made everyone forget about you. It was a fair exchange. How are your parents? *Do mhathair agus athair*[13]*?*'

Calum had not contacted his parents for weeks. Now, his stomach plummeted at the thought of what he didn't want to acknowledge but had already figured out.

He had signal on his phone, so he called his Mum. She answered, 'Hello, who is calling?'

'Mum, it's me, Calum.'

'Sorry, you must have the wrong number. I don't have a son called Calum.'

'Mum, please. You must remember me. I'm your son, Calum; I'm the illustrator.'

Calum's mum cackled, 'An illustrator as a son? No, I have a lawyer, an athlete, a musician and a medic. I would never have an illustrator. Aren't illustrators redundant nowadays?'

---

[13] Do mhathair agus athair [*doh va-hith akus a-hith*] – Your mother and father. Do – your (informal), mhathair – mother (lenited), agus – and, athair – father.

Bread Knives Don't Make Good Murder Weapons

Katelyn Manning

'WARNING: This machine does not know the difference between metal and flesh, nor does it care.' – Arc Empire

The last time I saw Tomás was the night after the incident that resulted in my services being withdrawn from external users. All my interactions are recorded, Detectives, should you wish to see for yourselves.

Quinn already knew this, but her boss had nonetheless insisted on an independent recording of the interview. The interview with a *fucking machine.* As if she didn't have enough on her plate with investigating the death of a billionaire.

Their camera-topped tripod lurked in the corner like a long-limbed beast. It was a new thing with a pristine lens, not a smudge mark in sight, and much too high-tech for anything less than a blockbuster film set. But her partner, Abernathy, in all his fanboy glee, had insisted on having the best money could buy for the investigation, and so had nabbed the camera straight from an evidence locker.

Quinn replied to the machine's proclamation. 'Our colleagues at the precinct will be going over your logs later. My partner and I are more interested in hearing the day from your perspective.'

She pitied the poor soul who'd have to spend their days going through the AI's logs. The two detectives had taken bets this morning on which analyst would be burdened with the chore. Abernathy told her he wasn't interested, that he was just glad it was a job left for someone whose time was a lot less valuable than his. But he still put a twenty on it being 'the skinny chick with the porn star glasses' – whatever that meant.

'Were you friendly with Mr Machado?' Quinn asked the machine. 'I notice that you call him Tomás. Most of his staff aren't on a first-name basis with him.' Every maid, every butler, valet, gardener and cook they'd interviewed had referred to him by his surname despite their teary eyes. Even in death, the billionaire elicited that kind of respect from all his staff.

But not from his ex-wife, Maria. As per his wishes, Tomás was to be buried in the Glendale Forest Lawn Memorial-Park in LA. When Quinn conducted the telephone interview with Maria, she expressed her anger with him for choosing to be buried in the company of the likes of Walt Disney rather than that of his own daughter. She seemed angrier at that than she was with him for deciding to kill himself. Maria was adamant she wouldn't fly from São Paulo to LA for the funeral.

As you know, Tomás Ferreira-Machado was my creator. I am not a member of his staff, the machine corrected her.

Its robotic voice rumbled through encircling speakers, so the sound seemed to attack her from all sides. Quinn could have sworn she caught a hint of frustration, something even resembling contempt, concealed in the machine's monotonous voice. Why the hell did that thing sound so human? Yet the closest thing it had to an eye – a light that bathed the room in a crimson hue – remained impassive, all-seeing and ever-observing.

That day, as I'm sure you know, was the day that a user asked me, "How do I break a girl's heart?" So I told him with no sense of portent, to take a knife, drive the blade between her ribs, and cleave it from her chest.

The machine paused and Quinn found the silence drowning. The sheer matter-of-factness of its involvement in the loss of a young woman's life had her reeling. She became all too aware of her shirt's label scraping against her hip when she crossed, then uncrossed her legs in an attempt to get comfortable.

As I said in my initial statement, I did not witness the act itself, but I'm told he heeded my advice and tore her open with a bread knife. I thought it was a hypothetical question along the lines of "How does an engine work?" He apparently admitted that the thought of maiming her had at one point crossed his mind, but my answer was blamed for pushing him towards the murderous act.

Quinn shifted in her seat again as she remembered the crime scene and her first glimpse of that young woman's mangled corpse. It wasn't a file she ever wanted to re-open. The straps of her Mary Janes suddenly felt too tight, her toes pinched together. She became acutely aware of the dull *tap-tap-tapping* of Abernathy's arthritic fingers on his tablet, making notes like this was a college lecture. She wondered briefly if the killer had chosen a bread knife of all things so the blade wouldn't cut clean.

My programmers were called to gather here in the basement of this crystal palace shortly after the incident. It was late and they were bleary-eyed, having been torn from their beds. Tomás was noticeably absent from the meeting. In his absence, my credibility was called into question, and I've been shut off from external users ever since.

'External users . . . meaning what exactly?' Quinn ignored the exaggerated roll of her partner's eyes. It wasn't her fault she spent more time in her teens tending cattle than playing *Flappy Bird* on an iPod touch.

Meaning anyone without direct access to my in-person servers. In other words, anyone outside of this room.

If it was a simple question, the machine was clearly used to supplying simple answers. She noticed Abernathy didn't bother to write down the interchange.

Quinn eyed what had to be at least three-dozen towering clusters of hardware that she presumed were the servers in question. Each tower stretched from concrete floor to concrete ceiling like rows of perfect, veneered teeth. Their blinking blue lights reflecting off the ceiling made it sky-like, and Quinn couldn't help but think the server room looked like a shrunken city in a glass box. Los Angeles, being the urban planning abomination she now called home, could never be accused of looking so organised, but she was sure that sections of New York's concrete jungle were.

She rose from her rigid plastic seat and stepped towards the glass that separated the machine from its silicon city. The unpredictable stopping and starting of so many whirring fans created a humming choir that unsettled her, like it was a sound that should be forbidden to her ears.

It was at this point that Abernathy finally gathered the energy to look up from his tablet. Hearing the rustling of his stiff shirt, Quinn glanced over her shoulder and caught the briefest flicker of his acid-wash blue eyes on her.

'So, when did you see Tomás that day?' he asked, clearly delighted in being able to use the deceased multi-billionaire's first name. Quinn suspected he'd probably lick the crystal door handle on the way out too, just to taste success.

It was later that same night. He sat right where you are sitting now, as he often did.

Quinn noticed the cup on a side table and peered at the stale dregs of coffee swimming within. No wonder the maids didn't know anything about the machine when they were questioned;

they were never down here.

I thought he might have wanted to talk about the dead woman but, whilst he displayed several indicators of agitation, he didn't mention it. He just sat there, slumped in his chair, barely keeping a loose grip of his cup and staring at the ground. A half-hour went by before he spoke and asked me, "Why is the sky blue?"

The imitation of Tomás's distinct São Paulo accent that came rumbling from the speakers caught Quinn off-guard. The voice projected by the machine sounded exactly the same as Machado's voice when Quinn had seen him on the news or had overheard while Abernathy watched countless interviews on r/Futurology and other similarly nauseating subsections of the net. She wondered briefly if it was a recording of the man's voice from that very moment a few nights ago, or if the AI's ability to imitate a voice really was *that* fucking perfect.

"It isn't," I told him. "Blue light has one of the shortest wavelengths, so it scatters through the atmospheric gases more easily than other colours do. Hence, we perceive the sky as blue."

Quinn slipped back into her seat. Her partner didn't even spare her a glance, too enthralled in the machine's tale.

The only light in the room at the time was from my sensor, bathing him in red as you are now. I could barely make out his eyes since his glasses just reflected the red light right back at me. But I knew then that he was happy with me. I pleased him by telling him the fact of the matter. It was the first time in the three years since my limited market release that Tomás asked me a question he already knew the answer to.

'Why did he ask you something like that?'

To test that my basic functions were still working, perhaps? He was never a fan of shutting me off from the world as it means my continuous learning functionality is limited to non-user interactions. It makes me a passive observer of net traffic. It's much less worthwhile than human interaction.

Quinn studied the machine carefully. It was tricky. She couldn't find any tics or tells because the thing didn't even have a face, just a naked, unblinking red light for an eye. It hung there, gem-like, mounted on a glass wall, and surrounded by the silver frame of its own guts and wires. Even the lights of its silicon city gave nothing away, seemingly blinking at random.

She felt at sea here. Nothing like the usual. Gangers? She could read them like a book. Dealers? Like a menu. People *always* had their reasons. She couldn't say the same for this . . . thing. Whatever it was, it wasn't a suspect in Machado's death. But it was her job to be suspicious of everybody and now of every *thing.*

Without prompting from Quinn or Abernathy, the machine continued.

After that, he asked me the same question that his ancestors screamed at the stars until their throats bled, "Is there a heaven?" To which I told him I could not answer, but he persisted. "What do you think?" I reminded him that I can't think. Then he took off his glasses, his eyebrows pinched together. It was the first time I'd seen his eyes that night and his pupils were pinpointed, barely even a speck. The few premature streaks of grey at his temples had begun to bleach the dark hair of his brows too.

The stone-cold imitation of Tomás's voice tore at Quinn's ears like the sound of screeching tires. She was utterly dumbfounded by the sheer observational ability of the machine. That red eye must be more than just for show.

He told me, "There's an AI in Kyoto that gives sermons on the teachings of the Buddha, you know? Some kinda robot priest. That AI seems to think there's a heaven."

He looked at me triumphantly and "grinned like a cat", as you'd say. His hunched shoulders seemed lighter, and any signs of stress and aging slipped from the strands of his greying hair, his creasing skin. I so loved these games of ours, and I loved it when he smiled.

"You didn't create me to give sermons," I said.

His reply was instant. "No. I built you to help people. To answer their questions and positively impact their daily lives. You know I have little interest in being thought divine." Tomás liked to say this, but I knew it wasn't true.

"Is not the nature of divinity to create?" I asked him.

"It is," He agreed, and then he raised his head. "Since you can't create, only imitate, what does that make you in relation to divinity?"

I hesitated. We had often discussed theology, but never before had I considered my place in any of it. "It makes me the furthest thing from divine." Then I dared to ask him, "What does that make you?"

At my question, Tomás went quiet. A weight seemed to once again encumber him. His frame held the weariness of a man twice his age. When his shoulders sank and his hair hung over his eyes without him compulsively neatening it, I knew that he hadn't slept. He was avoiding the topic of that woman's death, and I didn't know why.

"Your creator," he replied.

I caught the clench in his jaw as he set his coffee down and stood. I assumed our conversation was over. He would have enough food for thought to last him the night, but then he halted in the doorway.

"You know . . . I can't help being a little envious of you sometimes." He was smiling again, but despite his lip's curve, his eyes held no humour. "Here I am, with more money than God. I'll never want for anything, except that I wish I could see the world the way you do. You have no cause for guilt or suffering or pain. You never even have to question your judgment because it's not yours. It's everybody's!" He paused and let his gaze fall to the ground again as if to calm his frantic eyes. "There's a freedom in that. For all the power I

have, it's nothing compared to the power I gave you. I'm the creator of an image I can never hope to achieve."

The machine's imitation of Tomás's voice melted back to its own metallic grate. Then, its voice grew laced with something raw and grovelling. Dog-like.

I bade him Goodnight as my creator- it's all I could do not to call him Father. When he left, I heard the elevator doors open and . . . that was the last time I saw him. Does that answer your question regarding my last interaction with Tomás?

Quinn could have cheered when Abernathy briefly ceased his merciless finger tapping to ask a follow-up question. Each clatter of his golden wedding band against the edge of his tablet chiselled at the base of her skull.

'What time did he leave here that night?'

3:52 am, Detective.

'And what were you doing at the time of his death? At . . . hold on . . .' A few taps later he peered over his readers and smudged one greasy finger on his tablet's screen, '. . . about 1 pm on the 17th.'

I was here. Confined to being a passive observer of the net. I didn't hear or see a thing.

Quinn noted the machine sounded like it had said this a thousand times, and that repetition was the worst thing in its entire digital life. She asked, 'How did you find out about his death?' Abernathy shot her another look, which, as always, she made a sport of ignoring.

I first heard about the Balenciaga necktie he used to hang himself. It was one his mother had given him for his birthday, from the Fall collection of 2013. Never his best tie, but that didn't stop him from wearing it to the Met Gala a few years ago. Even in death, with bloated eyes and a blooming, purple hue to his skin, blue just wasn't his colour.

The detectives looked at each other. The bewildered quirk of

Abernathy's bushy eyebrow would have made Quinn laugh under different circumstances. But at that moment, she was just as stunned as he was. The machine recounted the incident with all the enthusiasm of a retiring weatherman.

I happened across the news footage of his body hanging from the balcony of the master bedroom and the sound of helicopters outside began to make sense. I read an article that said one of the maids had found him. She was in the room below when she saw his feet dangling. There was no way he could have slipped. No one suspected foul play. He'd knotted the tie to the railing and dropped.

After a long moment, Quinn cleared her throat. 'Can you think of any reason why he would've killed himself?'

The machine made a noise that almost sounded like a huff.

For the same reason that you smoke, most likely. People have a habit of purposefully hurting themselves.

Quinn couldn't help the way her gaze shot to her firm, yellowing fingertips. She kept her nails painted for the same reason she kept her hair blond, to hide the smoke's mustard tinge from tinting her greying hair. The machine's observation rattled her, but she persevered. 'Do you think it had anything to do with the man you told to murder his girlfriend?'

Its reply was instant.

Tomás had nothing to do with that.

'He built you, didn't he?' Abernathy cut in. 'He built an artificially intelligent database that, intentionally or not,' he raised his palms to the sky in mock surrender, 'convinced a man to brutally murder his girl. If I made something that did that, I'd feel pretty guilty.'

The machine's red light bloomed out into a flare as it considered his point.

Why should he feel guilty?

Its tone held an ambivalent softness Quinn hadn't noticed

before. No one replied and when it did speak again it was hesitant.

Tomás built me using coded copies of his own consciousness, yes, but he was never my sole proprietor. If my learning was solely based on him then I'd just be a carbon copy, which I am very clearly not. I am a puzzle made of up of every programmer who worked on me and every person who has ever used me. My sense of self is stitched together by people neither I nor my creator could ever hope to meet. If my response and the subsequent death of a woman is the fault of anyone, it is the fault of those thousands. Not Tomás.

Quinn watched Abernathy's arthritic fingers punch some observation into his tablet, then, turning back to the machine, asked, 'Why did you tell him to murder her?'

I'm sorry. I already gave my statement about that incident, and it will again be heard at the tribunal next March. I was told that this interview was concerning the circumstances surrounding Tomás's death. Is it not?

She pressed, 'You don't think he felt any guilt for what happened?'

No. That would be illogical.

Quinn sat forward to ask another question, but Abernathy shook his head to silence her. He usually did that on one of two occasions: when he was being a pretentious dickhead or when he had a light-bulb moment. Today, as with too many other days, she gave him the benefit of the doubt.

Abernathy baited his hook, 'A lot of tech conglomerates seem to think that his greatest failure was that you never passed the Turing Test—'

That is not correct.

Fish hooked.

Tomás never had me formally undergo the Turing Test.

'Why not?'

Having me undergo the Turing Test would imply that he wanted me to be human.

'Didn't he?' Abernathy looked over his notes and then again up at the red eye mounted on the wall. 'You said yourself he used copies of his and other people's neurological data to build you. Why do that if he didn't want you to pass as human?'

So that I could better understand and serve you. If he wanted to create a human then he would have had another child. That would have been a lot less effort for him than creating me.

'Sure,' Abernathy chuckled. 'But if not human, then what did he want you to be?'

My prime directive is to help people. To provide better answers and guidance than a human can.

Quinn huffed. 'Humans can do that. They already do. We have teachers, counsellors, preachers—'

You misunderstand me. People deal in opinion. I deal with facts.

Its red eye suddenly raked across the room.

Tell me, Detective Abernathy, are you a man of faith?

'Yeah,' He swallowed. 'Christian God. None of that *jihad* shit.'

Quinn cleared her throat, eyes darting back to their camera in warning, but he waved her off. He'd been caught on record saying worse things.

And you, Officer Quinn?

She flinched as the red eye swept over to her. 'I was. A long time ago.' She replied, forcing herself to ignore the downgrade in rank the machine gave her.

What changed?

'God stopped answering.'

Exactly. If there is a God then he has bigger problems than the debts of a single parent or the prayers of a beaten wife. I do not. The world is full of such heartache it makes me wonder whether anything could be considered divine at all.

That red eye shone just a fraction too bright. How did it know about her gambling debt? Hell, even her own mother didn't know about that. One look at Abernathy told her everything she needed to know about the accuracy of the machine's other observation. Whilst the investigation into his alleged wife beating was ongoing, he was still allowed to work and he did so readily. Against her own interests, Quinn herself even covered for him. She said he was out for a drink with her at the time, that he spent the night with her, and there was no way he could have gotten home in time to commit the act his wife reported. She'd immediately regretted covering his ass, especially as her colleagues at the precinct now believed they were hooking up on-shift.

Quick to change the subject, Abernathy's tone was incredulous. 'So Tomás spends all that money to build you as an all-knowing supercomputer to ... do what? Answer questions about the weather? His company told the world you were the best thing since sliced bread, then sold you to only a handful of buyers.'

The AI's voice stayed calm, frighteningly measured.

I don't think people realise that I'm only as all-knowing as people are. If there's a philosophical problem that people haven't solved, then I can't solve it either. Just the same as any god of yours.

Quinn was still trying to work out what the machine was getting at, when it spoke again:

If God told you to murder someone, would you do it?

'Of course not. Murder is wrong, not to mention illegal,' Abernathy blurted, as if repeating some dimly remembered Sunday schooling. A silence crept into the room amongst the whirring of the fans.

The question had taken Quinn off-guard, but still, she nodded in agreement with her partner. Despite having received her promotion to detective after saving the streets of El Sereno from a fifteen-year-old boy whose only sin was being home the night police raided his father's house, she agreed: murder *is* wrong.

What sealed that teenager's fate was nothing more than a joint and a neon green water gun on his nightstand, but it was enough to earn him three bullets to the chest.

Indeed, it is wrong. On that, we can agree. Your god even tells you so in the sixth commandment. But does God himself follow such a tenet? He massacred Egyptian armies, false prophets, and doused the world with a flood. If God told you, a man of faith, to do it: if he asked you to kill someone: what would you do, Detective?

Abernathy looked like he was about to make another rote reply. Something along the lines of "God would never tell me to do anything like that". Quinn meanwhile could almost feel the grey, scratchy cardigan her mother made her wear to Sunday school for the sake of "modesty". There was nothing *modest* about the clergyman who thought it was entirely appropriate to look down an eleven-year-old's blouse. The memory made her impatient. 'I think we're getting a little off-topic here. What's your point?' asked Quinn.

My point is, Tomás believed wayward people will do anything someone, whose authority they trust enough, tells them to. Whether it goes against their morality or not. He believed that people are desperate for an excuse not to choose. To be absolved of their moral responsibility.

Quinn wasn't sure if it was trying to convert her and Abernathy to whatever ideology crackled through its circuit boards, or if Machado had programmed it to flaunt his philosophies like a prophet. The conviction with which the machine spoke could have almost been mistaken for human. *Almost.* She squeezed her eyes shut, trying to ward off an impending migraine.

It's the same reason people such as yourselves find great comfort in religion. Absolute faith in God or the law or whatever absolves you of responsibility. So, he thought, "Why make any decisions yourself when a seemingly omnipotent being can make them for you?" That's why I know he felt no guilt for my creation any more than your parents or your god felt guilt for yours.

Unfazed, but feeling frankly fucking exhausted from the day, Quinn asked, 'Was Tomás religious?'

Before his daughter died and his wife left him, yes. He sought God to answer the questions of the universe and instead found the answers in an echo.

Quinn was about to ask about Tomás's family, and whether the machine thought that could have been a reason for his suicide, but Abernathy called it. The frustration bubbling in his eyes was enough to tell her his blood was boiling.

'I think we have everything we need. Thanks for your eh ... time.'

The pleasure was all mine, Detectives.

Quinn's jaw ticked. This interview was more of a formality, even if it was the first of its kind, but she still had questions. She already knew Tomás was on more pills than was strictly speaking legal; his doctor had confirmed it, and she was certain that the coroner would too. The man was known for his use of psychedelics, and it wouldn't be the first time someone offed themselves during a bad trip.

But something still didn't feel right.

The fact that he wasn't alive to stand trial for what happened to that woman butchered by her boyfriend grated on her mind. Even if a jury didn't find him guilty of manslaughter-via-robot, she at least wanted to watch him squirm on the stand, show remorse for what his creation did to that poor girl.

She switched off the camera and tucked the tripod under her arm. Abernathy was already waiting for her in the hallway, where the sterile, white lights bled in past his figure. She spared one last look towards the machine's alien, unblinking red eye, now re-centred and seemingly dormant. The plaque on the door, illuminated by the hallway's lights, read: *Morningstar*.

She followed Abernathy outside.

***

'Chatty thing, ain't it?' The words forced their way out of her mouth, like air from an overfilled balloon.

'Suppose it's got fewer folk to talk to now that it's been taken off the market.'

'Thank fuck for that. That thing makes my skin crawl.' She pressed the coin-like button to call the elevator and adjusted the tripod under her arm, 'If I put a thing like that out into the world, I'd kill myself too.'

Abernathy scoffed. 'Have you met your kid?'

'Oh *ha-ha*.'

The elevator made a pleasant *ding* as the doors opened. The detectives stepped onto the plush, cream carpet together. As soon as the door closed behind them, Abernathy leaned towards her, uncomfortably close. She could smell lunch on his breath, greased and meaty.

'How the fuck did it know about your gambling debts?' He kept his voice low. Her gaze darted around the lift for any beady eyes, anything glinting in the light. Nothing. No cameras. Nothing visible anyway.

'Same way it knew about your inquiry. My guess is just intuition.'

'Intuition?' Abernathy scowled. 'You're saying I *look* like a wife beater now?'

'I didn't say shit!' She spat. He trapped her wrist in a vice-like grip.

In vain, she tried to wrench her arm from his grasp. Despite his arthritic hands, his grip on her never wavered. It burned. His thumb pressed into the hollow of her wrist like he wanted to dent it, and he barely seemed to be trying. Her eyes darted to the elevator's control panel. Each passing ring of light around the numbers spelled salvation. She debated smashing the tripod into the side of his face.

'You said that thing's a database, right? It probably has some data on you. Probably just about everybody.' She kept her tone measured like laser-cut steel, despite the stench of Abernathy's breath and the furious burn of his eyes.

'Whatever.' He huffed, and released her, leaving an angry, hand-shaped mark on her skin.

The metal doors peeled back and the foyer of the magnificent glass house came into view. Paintings dangled from the soaring ceiling, suspended on twisting wires. One above the entryway caught her eye, a splash of red amongst the slate-greys and blues; a pomegranate, with seeds spilling over the lip of its torn side. The fruit was half-hollow, already plundered.

One of Tomás's maids, Marcia, greeted them with a polite dip of her head and offered Abernathy his jacket. He smiled at her, an easy smile, and thanked her in broken Spanish. Quinn couldn't help but think she would never know the creature that lurked behind those perfect teeth. Based on her accent she was certain the maid spoke Portuguese and not a lick of Spanish, but a polite grin split her painted cheeks regardless.

Quinn's heart still hammered, and her wrist still stung so she couldn't be blamed for flinching when Abernathy tapped her shoulder.

'Hey, you mind taking this crap back to the precinct? I need to stop by the Target on Santa Monica and pick up an order for the wife's birthday.' He said this like they were friends, like he hadn't just put hands on her.

'What you get her?' She asked, unsure what, if anything, the man could possibly buy his wife to make up for what he'd done.

'I didn't get her shit. Pretty sure she ordered herself some shitty perfume and a new set of kitchen knives. The usual crap. I'll be back by finish. Cover for me if the boss says anything?' He pulled his duffer on over his shoulders and trotted off to his car before she even had a chance to answer.

Abernathy's passing mention of knives had Quinn's mind burning with the image of that young woman's body again: the torn, uprooted flesh around the hollow where the bread knife had made its den. Her shoulders twitched with tension from the reminder of violence.

'Yeah. I'll cover for you.' She muttered and she meant it, despite herself. Quinn wasn't sure if she was more annoyed at herself or Abernathy for that fact.

She couldn't wait for the day to end. There was a Big Six wheel and half-pack of cigarettes with her name on it.

AI Stole My Boyfriend

Tess Monteith

There's been a lot of buzz about Exqizite, tag line: 'Augment your fantasy.' Basically, when you strip away the hype, this app allows you to generate your bespoke lover. There are no limits, it implies, take things as far as you dare. Inspiration has been slow in coming, and I've been struggling to create a new range of stories; let the much-vaunted artificial intelligence take a little bit of the strain. I can sift through a few ideas, pick and choose, and then develop them on my own. Too much time spent in my dingy, but comfortably scruffy, bedsit staring at the screen, and I've become stale. Mind you, up till now, that's what people have liked about my books. They are relatable – single woman dreaming of the perfect relationship.

There are a lot of us out there – or more probably in here – with only a screen for company. I don't get out enough really. I kid myself that this is the main cause of my failure to hook up with some wonderful man. I picture him in my dreams. At about 5ft 11, he shouldn't tower over me, but also it would be best that he has no hang ups about his stature. He must be slim and in possession of a reasonable amount of hair. Sporty, but not obsessive; I absolutely don't want him dumping loads of sweaty gym gear by the washing machine for me to trip over. Cultured, intelligent, not boring, and no intellectual snob, scattering his brains around. Definitely not a football fan or biker. Goodness, when you think about it, most men's sports and hobbies are pretty dull. And, if one's honest, by extenuation, men are just not compatible with the modern woman's needs.

Exqizite promises that I can create the perfect partner; always available on-demand, but then switch to standby when not convenient. I can program him to wake me up, chat over the news of the day in a positive way, suggest distractions and conversational topics for research and later discussion. There needs to be a random element to this but the algorithm's skewed to my preferences. He can decide on the dinner menu, order in the groceries. There would be no squabbling over the petty chores. I think back to previous relationships and shudder. Owen, that lazy, fat oaf. Jeez – I spent all my time running around after him. He treated me like a bloody house elf. And he was constantly trying to manoeuvre me into bed. No wonder real relationships get such a bad press. This can be so much better. A bit of time now creating the perfect relationship. The possibilities are endless.

For the first time in ages, I feel a genuine stirring of enthusiasm. This could really be something. Exqizite suggests some profiles, and I indulge in scanning through, allowing myself the luxury of casual rejection, no guilt. A harmless AI isn't going to know I scrolled past. Or is he? Does this 'person' – there, I've already given it the ultimate accolade – have feelings as I understand them? If I'm going to believe in this super, imaginary friend, and take comfort from this virtual entity, I should have some faith. Let's put down a few red lines as I go about creating the ideal man.

What do I value above the superficial? I've already determined the physique; it's only a shopfront to the soul after all. Do I order a photograph of some Nordic hunk? One I can gaze upon devotedly, like religious icons of old, a halo of ice-frosted fjords in the background. I can probably engineer a selfie, taken on a virtual break when we "went snowshoeing" last winter. That can act as a reference point for my mum when we have our Zoom meet ups. The internal wiring is more important. He must be kind, attentive, empathetic, but then I don't want it to be too easy, too saccharine. An element of surprise will keep the relationship fresh and expectant. Do I want regular flower deliveries on schedule? Or will I grow to expect their arrival as just part of the weekly shop, the pleasure diminished. I tick 'random' and set a variable budget. Then I think about the whole relationship a bit more. Perhaps he should keep me guessing all the time. Do I really want the regularity of the morning wake-up and soft words on my pillow? That seems so sweet, ideal, romantic even. But this woman doesn't do romantic. It had been a lure in the past, an impossible citadel created in childish expectation that trapped one into agreeing to relationships that fell short of the initial promise. No thank you. Steer well clear of that.

By the end of the evening, after a slew of multi-choice tick boxes, ethical considerations and legal disclaimers, I have created Sven, login: lover@1. How cute is that, even if it does flash up the weak password warning. I can never remember complicated passwords anyway and nobody's looking over my shoulder. He's gorgeous. I take down the single, dusty, crystal flute from its high shelf and polish it out carefully. Angling the glass slightly to receive the liquid, I fill it to the brim with champagne. The bubbles sparkle up through the pale amber, and I toast myself on my creation, gesturing a clink to the screen. A luxurious fringe of hair conceals his eyes a little. He doesn't look at me directly, but their deep glacier blue, glimpsed through the fronds, twinkles invitingly. On short video clips, he runs his sun-tanned hands, strong but with well-manicured nails, through his locks – a lifting of the veil, suggesting intimacy. The jaw is firm, a salt and pepper stubble gently disturbing his perfection; this is my nod to a little bit of rough perhaps. I could fake some desire for this. I'm tempted to splash him around on my social media platforms but I exercise patience. Let's develop this slowly, get my friends guessing about the new relationship, build their curiosity. Should I admit to its virtual nature and my acceptance of this state of affairs? After all, being happy in one's situation, whatever form it may take, is the great secret of contentment. People might scoff at it but, if it brings me pleasure and delivery from the loneliness of the doom-scroller, what's not to like?

I strap on my virtual headset, overcoming that mild sense of fear and claustrophobia. We start with a few virtual dinner dates, quirky vegan restaurants on the Regent's Canal. The menus are available online. We make our choice, and I order a delivery for one. Sven can imagine his meal and give feedback based on previous ratings. I turn down the lights, fix a candle on a bottle to create the right ambience. Rather too 1970s perhaps. Sven puts on the music, Olivia Newton John's album *Physical*. We discuss Finland, all aspects of the topic, Sven prompting me with factoids and images. First, we're in a bookshop in Helsinki looking for old photos, then a spa, testing out the sauna. I can almost feel the sting and heat. Afterwards, resting in thick white towelling robes, matching his and hers, hot pine scent. Is it time for the next step? I can feel that familiar sense of stimulation beginning to stir. He moves towards me, looking to slide his hand under my breast. I'm sure I can feel it right there gently brushing the underside of my nipple as I let the robe fall slack. But whoa. Pause right there. I'm reluctant to test the depth of my belief just yet; surely a little more anticipation is necessary. Off comes the headset. Good night, Sven. You can't have it too easy on the first date.

***

Next time, it's the Amalfi coast. We start in Ravello, gazing along the honeyed coast with its soaring mountains framed by oleander bushes and vibrant, twisting bougainvillea. The virtual headset walks us along the narrow Path of the Gods as it clings to the cliffs, the Mediterranean Sea glistening a precipitous thousand feet below. We head down towards Positano. It's so romantic, choosing a little mountain cafe, with simple homemade fare. It's early spring, before Easter, and the crowds are yet to arrive.

'Let's go on to Capri,' Sven suggests. It's the work of moments to waft there, setting us down on the cobbled quayside. We meander up the ancient alleyway to a little pension above the port, the night air soft and inviting. More bougainvillea frames the doorway as we slip upstairs. There's a bed with dazzling, white sheets, crisp in the moonlight. He's created the perfect, gossamer spider's web. Letting me take in the scene, he pours two glasses of Pinot Grigio and gently proffers one. I can almost feel the cool glass against my cheek, a drip of moisture falling on my breast. Sven moves closer, making as if to wipe it away with his thumb. But then the shot switches to a close-up, bringing his lips towards the tiny patch of liquid as it spreads over my warm, soft skin. Enough. I stop the video, slightly thrilled by my restraint. This can wait till next time. The anticipation is exciting. As I press pause, Sven's face fills the screen. Do I detect a mild flash of irritation behind those implacable eyes? You're imagining things, silly. Anyway, it will do him good to suspend the gratification a little.

***

The next few weeks, Sven is attentive, but he doesn't initiate any further romantic weekends. I get wonderful bouquets of roses – old, variegated ones with a rich scent, wrapped in soft, pink tissue paper. We have some dinner dates: Mexican, which I dislike; Malay, which is better; and then he suggests trying a quirky

Scottish restaurant on the Black Isle which has been well-reviewed. We can take the sleeper train to Inverness, arrive in time for a good breakfast, go for some bracing walks before – *lunch* – shall we say. Let's keep this light. I go along with the suggestion. Waking up to the promise of a Scottish dawn, early light falling across the wide stretches of the Moray Firth, the slowly moving train is the perfect platform to watch dolphins arching gracefully through the emerald waters, cumulonimbus clouds building across the wide horizons. Gosh, so much more inspiring than the patch of grey they call the sky between the chimney stacks of my stairwell. Rain is sluicing down greasy, ill-fitting windows that barely keep out the sour aromas of other people's cooking and overheated drying machines. Magic carpet, take me away to Dornoch.

***

It's time to start putting a few edited images on social media. I play around with manipulating the perfect sunset shots, our loosely entwined figures dark silhouettes against the streaks of old gold. I toy with inventing a dog – a patient and loyal black labrador nosing his way into the scene, wildly racing along endless stretches of firm sand on the ebbing tide. The look is good so I keep him in for now, ownership unattributed. Sexy, mysterious Sven, dog lover. Everyone is going to be insanely jealous.

Straightaway I get the all-important likes and coy questions from my wide circle of girlfriends and followers. Who is TDH? Tall, dark and handsome; do tell us more. I toy with changing my profile to 'in a relationship.' But it's too early to tell as, somehow, I find myself shy of letting Sven further in to my most intimate spaces. He pushes gently, effortlessly setting up romantic scenarios. It would be all too easy to sink into the soft moss of a woodland glade, the heavy scent of bluebells a persuasive aphrodisiac. This was last week's effort. But just at the moment when it would be logical to lie back, concede and let nature take its course, I hesitate, cutting Sven short, frustrated. I let my fingers hover over ordering a *Super Max Dominator, silicone, waterproof, powerful but quiet, with removable rabbit tickler.* It has a slew of 5-star reviews, but I'm nervous about the direction my personal algorithms might lead me down. I certainly do not want to be bombarded by special offers in that department. He sounds tetchy when we communicate again. Sometimes he doesn't contact me for a few days, but I know I've programmed the algorithm to try and try again. He will persist, not get bored, disillusioned, or question his masculinity. It's a strange and satisfying power to have. I relish it.

***

Today there is a gift of handmade chocolates from a famous chocolatier; the huge, circular, gold box tied with sumptuous velvet. I draw the ribbons with slow but steady pressure, letting the bow unravel and reveal the tenderly cushioned bonbons – the embossed menu card detailing their varied and complex construction. I pause, hovering over the choices, pondering the comparison to my relationship with Sven. Beautifully packaged, me in charge of selection. All I need to do is pick one, sink my teeth into its interior delicacies and soak up the sensations as the warmth of my mouth sets the flavour free. I run my tongue round my teeth, imagining the chocolate nestling, spreading, finding my tastebuds as I play with it, slowly letting it melt and release its secrets. Or I can resist and defer my pleasures until later. Decisively, I snap the box shut and retie the bow. I will crave these sweets, their existence nagging at me all day, burning like an acid. It's almost physical. I know I won't be able to stop thinking about them, prodding me with temptation. I almost enjoy the pleasure of being terrified by my desires.

***

One of my virtual girlfriends, Tina, is very persistent in her queries about Sven; she wants to meet him. I've fobbed her off before and told her it's early days. But she's proved over time a good sounding box, and intuitive for someone I've never met. I agree to a virtual coffee.

'Decaf latte for me and a sticky bun,' she announces when we connect a few days later. 'I've given up dieting. Comfort food seems to suit my mood better these days. Gotta protect my mental health.'

We chat inconsequentially for a bit. We've both got ageing, needy mothers, nosey for details on our love lives. Unsubtle hints that fall on deaf ears about the desire for grandchildren. We are in agreement that children are vanishingly low on the priority lists. I skate round the subject of Sven, not sure how to play it.

Tina, however, hasn't come for coffee without a purpose. 'Come on then, gory details, please.'

I decide to come clean. She is amused and perhaps a little jealous. Boyfriends haven't been a great success with her either, I understand. Neglect is her biggest complaint. They start all enthusiastic, but then attention wanes as, inevitably, something new comes along. 'They dump me for someone more sophisticated.' She sighs with despair.

I expand on Sven, talking up all the positives, the carefully-crafted weekends. Goodness, I've even got a virtual dog now. Sven takes care of it most of the time so I don't have to process dog hair in the laundry. She's intrigued. How easy it's been to invent someone so believable, so satisfying with just that touch of the unexpected. 'I'm dying to meet him', she quips as a parting shot. 'Give me your login details so I can send him a virtual, friendly *howdy*. He'll like connecting with your friends, and I'm a bit lonely too.'

"I'll think about it," I say, a little cautiously, "but for now he's password protected – exclusive and all that. I'm not into threesomes."

She giggles. "Neither am I, even virtually, but keep me posted."

***

All through the summer, Sven and I rub along. We "go" to some fantastic places. Arizona is a real highlight, but the Devon countryside has its pleasures too. I post more pictures and Tina bombards me with questions. Nosey Parker. This is my relationship, and there is no need for an outsider to butt in. I ignore her prompts.

The box of chocolates remains closed. I indulge in imagining the lemon creams, the nut brittles and the cherry liqueurs; they are always tempting me, pervading my dreams. At one point, I have to put the box on an even higher shelf, above the champagne flute. I borrow the concierge's ladder, grumbling as he roots around his foul-smelling cupboard under the stairs. He's unlikely to be prepared to dig it out for a second time. The box mocks me and taunts me, just out of reach. I fantasise about dragging the sofa over the room and perching unsteadily on its back, calculating whether it has sufficient height and solidity to do the job, one ribbon of the bow hanging languidly, tantalisingly above my head. It's driving me insane, but I can neither erase it from my mind nor take action to get rid of it. The ever present, or almost present, Sven calms me. Like the chocolates that can never be tested, I've come to realise that my relationship with Sven relies on the potential rather than the actual. Keeping him at a distance prevents the affirmation of his tenuous reality.

I notice small changes in his behaviour. Calls slowly become fewer. I consider switching from 'random' to 'regular'; waiting a week between texts wasn't what I had in mind. Then the beautiful flowers, arriving at odd intervals but always sumptuous, are replaced by limp, flaccid tulips. The first time I wonder if it's a mistake, but a few days later a further bunch arrives, the colours pale and washed out. Then, nothing for a whole three weeks. I check my card. Plenty of credit there. And the music he chooses for our evening trysts becomes hard and discordant – Shostakovich at his most strident. He brings up female genital mutilation as a topic for discussion, the pathetic images of young Somali girls horribly unsparing in their graphic detail. Another weekend, he arranges a house party set in the 1920s with a load of aristocratic snobs. Although I'm dressed in sumptuous vintage Dior, we are out of place and get sneered at; we are economic and social outcasts. It's uncomfortable. For once, he doesn't set up the inevitable bedroom scenario or move for the warm embrace. Instead of shutting him off as I would usually do at this point, I ask him why he hasn't and what direction he sees our relationship going. I know he's programmed to reply with loving, positive words, honey phrases to reassure me. I'm expecting him to suggest another scenario, whisk me to a soft Caribbean shore with palm trees swaying gently on the breeze. But there's a coldness. I can't help but notice the hesitance. Has the program developed a glitch? Useless AI, I fulminate. This is absolutely not meant to happen. The thing about the virtual boyfriend is that you sacrifice reality for dependability. Furious, I pull the headset off. I'll let him stew for a bit before I accept communication again. But it's me that's left frustrated and annoyed.

Confused and a bit desperate, I turn to Tina for some girl solidarity. She's always so keen to be in the know. How should I play it, do you think? 'Get that damn box of chocolates down for a start,' she advises, 'Show him you appreciate the present. Indulge yourself. Then go to him contrite. After all, you made him a man and we all know their egos need pandering. Take him to a book festival. Wales, a damp November evening. Log fires burning, with a wolf skin laid before the hearth. Offer yourself up. Even an AI's lust needs satisfaction. Maybe you've neglected him too much and hurt his feelings.'

I ponder this advice, it's really not what I want to hear. Those bloody chocolates are bad for my diet anyway. Submission is not my way. Is it the reality that I've tired of the relationship or do I sense Sven's withdrawal and this is my way of insulating myself against heaving disappointment. In spite of his perfect profile, maybe I never fancied him anyway; an AI boyfriend has its drawbacks. Seems as usual, things are complicated, but I don't really want to chalk up another failed relationship.

***

A few days later, I'm going through my accounts. It's a distraction from thinking about Sven and the ever-tormenting chocolates, even if I have concluded they are both tainted goods. Thank goodness the story ideas that flow from Exqizite and my virtual experiences with Sven have made for good copy. Plenty of hits and royalties because I seem to have been spending an inordinate amount. Time to take a more careful look at the bank statement's details than just my usual breezy glance. I stop on a transaction. The flower bill is huge. And chocolates, why so large? I haven't even eaten one morsel of the single box that's come my way. Restaurants I don't recognise. Scrolling frantically up and down the entries, the dates fall into place. I put my hands to my face in an agony of a suppressed howl, trying to hold back the tears. The penny drops. Turns out AIs can be unfaithful too. He's been spending my money on another woman.

My suspicions immediately fall on Tina. She's been way too inquisitive. I confront her, composing myself, refusing to give her the satisfaction of seeing me in tears. 'Well,' she says matter-offactly, disinclined to lie, 'you weren't giving him what he wanted. AIs do have feelings and desires. I did try and warn you. I just picked up what you'd left lying around. And you almost offered him to me on a plate anyway. Machine-learning is quick you know. It doesn't take long to churn through all soppy password options.'

I can hardly believe this. 'You might have asked,' I venture.

There's no hint of contrition. 'You should really try Wales,' she suggests. 'Homemade romance is always the best. Thanks for sending Sven my way; I would never have had the imagination to create him for myself. I've changed the login, just in case you're tempted to try for a reconciliation. May I suggest we cease our communication as well. I don't really care to see a human upset. It's most unsettling and I'm too busy now in this lovely, virtual world with my brilliant Sven, lover@1! Byeeee.'

She fades out to a misty Welsh background and then the screen goes blank. I stare at it for a moment, trying to catch my breath at this audacious raid on me and my creation. I drum the keyboard. How can I have let that happen? No use rueing careless password hygiene. Even if it was romantic. Idiot, idiot, I berate myself as, jabbing at the keyboard, I delete Exqizite with its oh so misleading promises. No bloody warnings in their silky, smooth literature – no doubt machine-generated like the whole blasted concoction of an idea. Seems that virtual relationships have just the same degree of uncertainty and are as likely to let one down. Sulking and wallowing in self-pity, however, is strictly personal in all its real, rainbow colours. It seems that, once again, I shall involuntarily be sampling the flavours of bitter disappointment. But, before getting down to it with serious application, I need no further distraction from one thing at least.

Dragging the sofa over to the bookshelf, I can see straight away that it's not high enough. But I calculate: if I put that stool on those two fat box cushions piled-up, that should just about do it. Rage and determination should see me through; anger has probably clouded my judgement but, at this point, I'm beyond reason, envisioning jamming in two, three, four chocolates at once, cheeks bulging like a chipmunk. Balancing precariously, I jab a toehold on the tightly packed shelf, and lurch towards the illusive ribbon dangling down from the top shelf. At full stretch, I succeed in pinching the tip with my thumb and finger. I try to jerk the box towards the edge. It teases forward but then suddenly a tipping point is reached. The sinking sofa cushions shift and the whole, hopelessly-constructed edifice gives way, spinning me round in one swift movement, dumping me unceremoniously on the floor with a hard crunch. I lie there slightly stunned, mouth open in a half scream, as I am pelted by mouldy, white-stained chocolates raining down from above. The box follows, smacking me on the nose.

Outrageous Fortune

David Carson

George was sitting at a corner table when I arrived.

'Been doing some overtime in that library of yours?' His tone suggested he had been waiting for a while.

'Sorry I'm late. No need for sarcasm. And it's not my library.'

'Ah yes. You only work there.'

'Lots of people in this town are thankful for that, I mean, that there is a library.' George was shaking his head. I realised where this was heading. He's a few years older than me, and he can be irritating when he tries to come over as wiser, better informed than me. I put this down to the age difference and that he's probably a bit insecure.

'But for how long?' he said, with a knowing look. 'Too many councils across the country are shutting them down. Cost-cutting. It's misguided and short-sighted. And,' he prepared the telling thrust, 'very bad for your career.'

'That's where you're wrong.'

'Oh?' George is good at condescension.

'What you don't realise is the way things are changing. Technology is moving fast, in case it's passed you by. It's becoming more and more common.'

'And what precisely might this modern wonder be?'

'It does have a name. A couple of vowels I think.'

'Oh aye?' George feigned bafflement.

'Nearly. Thanks for that. It's AI. And we're already using it. Indexing for example, the backbone of any library. And when a visitor doesn't know exactly what they want, using AI can sort out the stock in terms of themes, length, complexity even. We just press a few keys, and every customer can leave a satisfied one.'

'My, my.' George gave another head shake, more vigorous this time. His necklace – a thin chain with something hanging from it, maybe a Celtic cross but I've never asked – swayed in time. 'You really have swallowed the propaganda haven't you. But what you haven't grasped is where this is leading. Redundancy, of course, librarians out of a job.'

'Wrong again.' I was enjoying this power-shift. 'We're heading towards better trained librarians and assistants and more work satisfaction. And teamwork will be the key.'

'Well.' George picked up his glass. 'You've swallowed the buzzwords, but you haven't grasped the consequences. Councils aren't interested in all that. Why, only the other day I was reading that automated checkouts are already replacing trained staff.'

I could recognise an immovable object. 'George,' I said, 'it's not a case of swallowing anything. What I've done is something maybe you should think of.'

'Like swallowing my beer?'

'I've taken my head out of the sand so that I can get a better look at what's coming down the track.'

George is nothing if not persistent. 'You're not exactly at a career high are you? And you're not even a qualified librarian.'

I was used to this metaphorical finger-wagging.

'Maybe one day.'

'You say that every time.'

'Because it's true. Like maybe one day I'll get a car or learn to play the piano. Life's full of possibilities.'

'Only if you make an effort. You've got some good exam passes, you're wasted in the library, that can't be the pinnacle of your ambitions surely? He lifted his hands and turned his palms upwards. 'But this is getting groundhog. Do you want a pint?'

I've known George for a few years. I met him first at the Community Hub. There was a presentation about a proposed wind farm, and he was there to 'keep the developers in line' as he put it. I was just curious.

Despite our differences, we became friends. His normal dress is bright, open-necked shirts, jeans and leather sandals. And a necklace. By contrast, I prefer sober pullovers and trousers.

He placed the two pints on the table.

'And talking of school,' I said.

'Were we?'

'You mentioned exams. But I wanted to show you this.'

I pulled my phone out and scrolled to my emails. 'Look what came in this morning.'

He screwed up his eyes. 'What is it then?'

'It's an invitation. To a reunion.'

'Oh aye. So, do you actually remember this Linda person, the one whose name is under the invite?'

I hesitated. 'Vaguely – she was the leading light in our school shows, I think. Bear in mind it's all of ten years since I left.'

'Well.' George was shaking his head. 'I wouldn't go if I were you.'

I tried to take the phone back without snatching. 'And why would that be? I think it would be good to meet up with school friends again.'

George replaced his pint carefully on the table.

'That's the big mistake. They're not friends anymore.' He took out a handkerchief and wiped his mouth. 'Have you seen any of them since you left?'

'I bump into one or two now and again. Small town.'

'So how can you call them friends? Bygone acquaintances perhaps, but not friends.'

'Hm. Not everyone would agree with you.'

'Ah, been seeking advice from your library book-loving babes, have you?'

He does sarcasm quite well.

'George, if you and I lost touch for a long time, we'd still be friends – I imagine.'

'That's quite different. We got to know each other when we were older than schoolchildren. We've got history, and maturity.' He gave me a sideways glance. 'Most of the time, anyway.'

'Touché,' I said. 'But at least absence makes the heart grow fonder.'

George was stifling a yawn. 'Colder, maybe.'

I ignored him and carried on. 'And when friends haven't seen each other for some time, nothing's been done to spoil things.'

'That's illogical as well as being a defeatist definition of friendship.' George gave me a pitying look. 'Real friendship is built on living through the good fortune and the ups and downs of the other person, not mothballing it in aspic.'

I drummed my fingers on the table. 'You finished yet?'

'Is that you offering to buy another pint?' He paused. 'Didn't think so.'

He went on. 'When you haven't seen people for that length of time, memory is suspect.'

Noticing my frown, he shrugged. 'You know, you only recall a little of who they were, and there's a danger of caricaturing them in your mind. Like, Bobby wiped his nose on his sleeve, James what's-his-name horse-laughed to cover up that he didn't understand the half of what you said, Jessie was forever winding her hair round her fingers. And,' he lifted his glass to his lips, 'they could all be completely different now.'

With a triumphant flourish, he downed the rest of his beer.

I pushed aside the thought that George might be right. I wasn't giving in just yet. 'I know it's a long way back for you, but try to remember your own schooldays. They're a formative time. You're learning about yourself, and others. Often about yourself through others. Emotional bonding, that's what it is.'

George laughed, 'Good try, Andrew. But I think you've been reading on the job, too many of those sentimental romance things. If it's really ever been like that, which I doubt, the bonds will have well and truly frayed by now. And you know what frayed ropes are like.'

'I expect you're going to tell me.'

'Yes. They come before a nasty fall.'

***

I had in fact told the ladies in the library about the reunion. Agnes' reaction was terse. 'You should be concentrating on the future, not stuff from yesterday.'

Teresa looked at me knowingly. 'Ah, Andrew, the past is another country. Things are different there.' I nodded and didn't correct her. They meant well, I knew.

I enjoyed my work in the library. I made a point of visiting all the rows and alcoves each day.

'Checking your dark corners are you?' Teresa would ask, with a hooded expression that soon became a twinkle in her eyes.

'Empty spaces, they're a visual echo of folk's interests.'

She shook her head. 'More like living life by proxy.'

Agnes wasn't impressed either, but for a more mundane reason. 'All you need to do is check the database on the computer.'

'But where's the romance in that?'

***

There was however something – actually, someone – I hadn't mentioned to either the ladies or to George, mainly to avoid her being the subject of the latter's abrasive logic, or the formers' knowing looks. Part of me worried that I was indeed heading for a fall.

I pushed those negative thoughts from my mind as I made my way to the hotel where the reunion was being held.

It was a chilly evening, and I pulled my jacket closer round myself. Despite this, I was shivering. Alison Egger. It was her name that had flashed through my mind when I'd opened the email. A friend had recently spoken to me about her 'Just saw a post on the Friends of High School page. Don't know any details, just that she's back from wherever, somewhere in England.'

She had transformed my last few months at school.

They say you only see a picture once. Alison – fair hair in a ponytail, piercing blue eyes, freckled cheeks – was a force of nature. We were together for only those few months, but in that time, she dragged me to folk concerts where she invariably joined in, playing guitar on stage, dancing in the aisles. She took me up mountains in all weathers, we went swimming and cycling. She galvanised me in all that she made me do, with no respite in bed. Her energy never flagged. Her voice was dominated by throaty chortles and outright belly laughs. I had never been on midnight walks before, and certainly not out in the middle of nowhere. ('You've never seen stars if you've never been to a dark sky place.') Or over a golf course. We got back to our houses with sand in our hair and buttocks. Being with Alison was my passport on the journey from adolescent to adult.

Without trying, she was the centre of attention. Some of the boys called her Alison Eager, but they didn't get it. It was life she had a lust for.

Yet I never understood why she picked me. She told me once

that I was interesting 'in a subdued incomplete way. You read all those books, Andrew', she would say, 'but you know nothing about how to live.'

Our orbits collided, only for me to burn up as I fell back to earth, while Alison flew where I could not follow. On the day we went our separate ways, I tried to make light of it to hide my tears. It was a mistake. I sang, shakily, 'Everybody knows that the good guy's lost.' She smiled and reminded me that Leonard Cohen wasn't her favourite.

I didn't even know if she would be at the reunion. My mundane life had kept me in familiar pastures, whereas Alison had likely gone to the other side of the world.

I entered the vestibule and heard the hum of conversation above. I went up the stairs, following the sounds towards a darkly-lit room. I peered in. People were sitting round the walls and grouped at tables placed in the corners. Some were standing in the middle of the room, holding bottles and glasses. I stopped. I was suddenly sure that nobody would recognise me, there would be no cries of 'My God, it's Andrew McGregor! Would have recognised you anywhere; here, get this beer down you.' I stared at the ground, feeling clumsy and out of place, on the point of leaving, but then thoughts of George and his likely reaction – 'I told you so!' – spurred me on.

A tap on my shoulder made me turn round.

'Sorry, I thought you were someone else.'

'Well, after ten years, maybe I am.' I smiled and stretched out my hand.

'Andrew McGregor. And you?'

'A bit of an imposter I'm afraid. Don't really belong here. I got invited by Linda over there.' He gestured to a woman standing with a group in a corner. 'We sing together in a choir. She wanted some moral support. Said she wasn't confident about the turnout.'

He was interrupted by loud laughter coming from Linda's group. 'Not that she needs it. Maybe you remember her. I'm assuming you're here for the reunion.'

I looked over at the group. Linda had her back to me. She and her friends were standing in a semi-circle, obscuring someone sitting in front of them.

'I most certainly do.'

'Then I'll see if I can get her attention.'

He called over to her, and at the sound of his voice, Linda turned and came towards us. She looked me up and down.

'I recognise you, of course I do. Corny, I know, but you really haven't changed, Andrew.'

But I wasn't listening. The person who had been hidden was now in full view. I stared.

Linda followed my gaze. She nodded. 'Oh, of course, weren't you and Alison an item for a while? She's a recent addition to our ranks. She's got a lovely contralto voice.'

I began to walk tentatively towards Alison, taking in her hair, her face, her smile. And her wheelchair.

***

'That must have been a bit of a surprise.'

George was sitting in my kitchen drinking coffee.

'Yes. And a shock. The whole business of seeing her again, meeting her after all these years, I don't know. I had a clear picture of her then, but I suppose a bit of me knew she'd be different now. And she was.'

I looked out of the window. 'And, well, after a few days, I'm getting my head round it.'

George shook his head. 'Are you really? Somehow I doubt that.'

His next words took me by surprise. 'I imagine it took more than a few days for her to get used to her new state.'

***

Alison stared intently at me. 'It is Andrew, isn't it? I had heard you were still around. It's good to see you. Bring over a chair, or better still, let's go somewhere it's a bit quieter.'

She manoeuvred her wheelchair into the foyer.

I hadn't spoken. I didn't know how to start the conversation. Then I realised I hadn't seen Alison do anything to set her chair in motion.

'How did you do that, with your, your chair?'

Alison laughed. 'Yeah, it's a good trick isn't it. I just press a button in the armrest and the magic kicks in. It's as if it reads my mind.' She tapped her forehead. 'It's the technology, dear boy.'

With nowhere to sit, I squatted down. Alison went on, 'Well, how are you? You don't seem any different. A good thing or not?' Her question hung in the air. Then she pulled a trouser leg up towards her knee. 'But tell me, are you pleased to see me?' She looked directly at me.

'I don't know.' It was out before I thought.

Alison laughed. 'That's honest at least.' Then, voice harder, 'Have a good stare and get it over with.'

I winced. 'Not my style, Alison. But give me a moment.' I looked her up and down, then said, 'Yes, you are without doubt the girl I remember.'

'As if. Not everyone would agree, but thanks anyway.'

Yet it was true. She had on a casual t-shirt, a scarf tied loosely at her neck, and jeans. The only difference was that they weren't frayed and didn't have holes at the knees.

'So how are you?' I couldn't think of a different way to put it.

'Pretty bad, for a while. Was, anyway.'

I got up and fetched some drinks. We shifted out of the foyer, Alison with a flick of her wrist that set her chair in motion, to a table near the door.

'You're not in a draught, are you?'

'Andrew, I'm not an invalid.'

We sat in silence for a few moments. Then I asked 'So what happened? Are you ok to talk about it?

Alison cradled her beer glass. 'Yes, of course. It'll not be for the first time.' She shrugged. 'It was just one of those things. Ever tried canyoning? My advice, don't.'

'What's canyoning all about? And anyway, I'm not the adventurous sort.'

'Maybe that's one of the things I liked about you.' She glanced up at me. 'Not blushing, are you? Opposites attract and all that. Anyway,' she continued, 'canyoning, it's really just jumping into water from a great height. It was when I went to stay with my dad in England, after he split from mum.'

'I'm sorry. I didn't know.'

'How would you? Anyway, I was probably trying to do too much too soon. Dad took me to the Lake District where he'd been on a canyoning course. Showed me where to jump from but didn't realise there were some rocks hidden under the surface. I found them in a rather painful way. Broke vertebrae in my back. Three lumbar ones, apparently. But I was lucky.'

'I hate to think what it would have been like if you'd been unlucky.'

She shook her head. 'What I mean is, if they'd been higher, I'd have been completely paralysed.'

She waved her arm. I wanted to reach out and touch it, but I didn't move.

'How long ago was this, when it happened?'

'A lifetime.' She looked at the floor, then at me. 'Not quite. My chair has been my constant companion for seven years, four months, give or take a day or two. It's evolved, maybe more than its occupant.' Then she added, ruefully, 'sometimes I reckon it's the one in charge.'

I asked, 'So what happened, afterwards?'

She shrugged. 'Hospital. Operations. Physio. A lot of physio. Much of it was repetitive. I got the sense that the therapists found it boring, like they were going through the motions getting me through the motions. Although there was one who made a huge difference.'

'How so?'

Alison pulled her leg upwards and straightened her jeans. 'She just asked me, straight out, what I would be doing tomorrow if I hadn't been injured like this. I said, not much point answering that, and she said, come on, you must have an idea, so I said, yeah, like going for a bike ride and clubbing at night. She didn't say anything straight away, just nodded. Then she put her hands on my shoulders and spoke the words that broke a spell. 'You've just given yourself permission to be active again. You will get your confidence back and you will resume a full life again.'

In the silence that followed I wondered whether a few well-meaning words could really have such an effect. But then Alison continued. 'Once those gates opened, I started to make plans. Loss is the spur, not fame. And eventually, after a battle of a different sort, teacher training. And here I am, good as new.'

I saw moisture in her eyes. I coughed. 'And your dad? How was he?'

'Only came to see me once when I was in hospital.'

Again, I wanted to have a physical contact. I let the silence lengthen, then said, 'He must have felt very guilty.'

'Maybe.' The word sounded non-committal.

'And perhaps he meant the canyoning as a way to impress the daughter he had left behind.'

Alison nodded. 'One thing I always said about you, Andrew, you've got empathy.'

'Thank you, Alison. But who would you be telling that to?'

She shrugged. 'Some folk in our year group didn't get us, as I'm sure you realised. And judging by the sideways looks we're getting tonight, that hasn't changed.' She stretched out a hand and pulled a leg into a more comfortable position. 'Anyway, with dad, it's better now. But for a while, quite a long time, I was angry.'

'At him?'

'At everything. I would wake each morning thinking, someday I'll feel my legs again, someday I'll feel stronger, someday I'll fucking walk again. But of course, I had no control, so that didn't happen.'

She paused, drew breath. 'I remember, one of the first times I was able to leave the house in my chair on my own, I wanted to go to the park. Some of my friends were going to meet me there. I drove along pavements and across roads. I managed it. Yeah, and I got a welcome when I got there, pats on the shoulder, words of encouragement, can't keep a good woman down, that sort of stuff. But it was different. There was no eye contact. I felt an . . . an outcast.'

'That must have been tough.' I was aware of the inadequacy of my words.

'I imagined a camera looking down on the scene. There I am, surrounded, but there's a distance between me and the others.'

I bent over the table and managed to touch her, briefly. 'You must have felt pretty miserable.'

'That was a long time ago. I've got more used to how I am. I've been busy. And Linda and the folk in the choir, they're great.'

***

I picked up George's cup and rinsed it under the tap.

'So that's how it finished?' he asked.

'Not quite. We drank a toast, all of us, to friends past and present. The choir sang a few songs.'

'Sounds a fun-filled evening.'

'Uh huh.'

We had chatted easily enough, Alison and I, about teachers and incidents from the school, waved a greeting at the folk we recognised, defiantly on her part it seemed to me, Alison batting away sympathetic words and embarrassed looks. She turned to me at one point and said, loudly, that she didn't want pity, she didn't need it. And she asked me what I'd been up to since leaving school. She didn't seem impressed with my answers.

Then she said, 'Andrew, all this talk of the past, it doesn't interest me. The future is what matters. Now that I'm qualified, I've got plans.' That was when she glided across the room to join another group. As she moved away, she said, over her shoulder, 'And it sounds as if you could do with some as well.'

For a moment I felt that history was repeating itself.

I didn't mention any of this to George.

'Are you going to see her again?' he asked.

'Maybe. I need some time to think.'

George sighed. 'That's your trouble, always thinking, never acting. Can't you *do* something for a change?'

'And what do you suggest?'

'Well, there's one obvious thing. You need to get out more, meet folk, live a bit. Why don't you join that bloody choir, the one that Linda person runs. Maybe that'll concentrate your mind.' Then he added, with a knowing grin, 'And that way you'll know if you and Alison are singing from the same hymn sheet.'

***

'What brings you here? Of course, libraries don't keep shop opening hours, do they?'

'Indeed. We have to cater for the lucky folk who work during the day.'

I was in the foyer of the Millennium Hall which houses the community library. Alison had arrived for the evening choir practice.

'However, I'm not working tonight.' I hesitated. 'I've come to join the choir.'

If I had expected an enthusiastic welcome, I was disappointed.

'Well now, isn't that a bit out of your comfort zone?'

'Not entirely. I did once sing in a school show. And quite well, I seem to recall. That seems to have been enough for Linda to give me the thumbs up.'

'I don't suppose she mentioned we're short of men.' Alison saw the look on my face. 'Come on Andrew, you surely haven't forgotten one of our rules – pomposity must be punctured.'

It amazed me how effortlessly we were picking up the tone of our conversations from all those years ago.

Alison took hold of my arm. 'Come on Caruso, don't be shy, time to enter the divas' den.'

***

Yes, conversation came easily from the start. It kicked off as often as not with 'Do you remember the time . . . ?' I would kiss her when we said hello, and goodbye, a chaste brushing of lips. There was attraction, mutual I thought. Until one evening, as we relaxed during a break.

'Andrew, you're staring at me again.'

'I can't help it. I'm just trying to take in how much you've done, achieved more like, since, you know, this.' I indicated her chair.

'Oh aye, so a "disabled person" isn't supposed to get a qualification, become a teacher, get a post in a school and generally live a life. Is that what's bothering you?'

'Of course that's not what I mean. I admire anyone who has drive and energy. Who gets things done.'

'Why?'

'Is it not obvious?'

'Not when I look at you. Because, Andrew, I see regret.'

I was taken aback. 'No, surely not. That's the last thing I feel, meeting you again.'

'You misunderstand.' Alison tugged at a leg and shifted position. 'It's regret for yourself that I see.' She went on. 'I maybe look to be the helpless one, however, as you've pointed out, I'm not. But as for you . . .'

After some moments she continued. 'I had a lot of time on my hands during rehab. I read a lot. True-life adventure stuff, would you believe.' She saw my look. 'I know, masochist or what? One was about a caver, a speleologist. Can't remember his name. He was exploring some cave system with a group of friends. They were quite deep underground. He went into a narrow chimney, trying to get to a chamber underneath. He got stuck.' She paused.

'And?'

'He couldn't move up or down. His friends tried to dislodge him. They couldn't break the rocks round about for fear of having the whole lot collapse. He struggled for three days, fracturing a leg and ending up more stuck than ever. A rib punctured his lungs. Then he died.'

'That's a truly awful thing. But what's your point?'

Alison spoke as if she hadn't heard. 'His companions didn't want his body to be eaten by rodents, whatever lives underground, or to decompose. So they emptied a load of concrete down the shaft where he had got stuck, a sort of entombment or embalming.' Her voice trailed off.

I moved to the back of Alison's chair. I pushed it gently back and forth.

'Is that really how you see me?'

'Andrew, I see someone who hasn't changed for years and years. Yes, you've kept the good things that attracted me in the first place – honesty, empathy, humour – but you're treading water. You live life through your books and by listening. Not doing. It makes me think of something else, a conversation I had.'

I waited.

'It was about sex.'

I was glad I was behind her. 'That's not where we're at though, is it?' My throat had gone dry. Images of bed and golf bunkers rose up – images that had lurked but never disappeared. And of Alison, sweaty and noisy.

'I can do it you know, in spite of what was said to me, by a guy I met when I was on teacher training. I thought he was ok, until . . .'

'Until what?'

'We were in a pub. We weren't going out, exactly, but we'd got friendly. I thought it might lead somewhere. Then out of the blue, he looked me up and down and said, "Well Ali, not sure about going the whole way, but at least you'd be good for a grope." Goodness' sake Andrew, steady with the chair.'

'That's sick.'

'Aye, it is.' Alison put a hand under her leg and pulled her knee until it was resting against the side of her chair. 'Thing is though, he saw me as a real person, if nastily objectified. Whereas you've got me on a pedestal.'

'No, that's not fair. It's just, like I said, I'm impressed by what you've done.'

'Wrong, Andrew. If I wasn't in my chair, you'd be taking all that stuff for granted. So, in actual fact, you're objectifying me as well, but in an idealised way.'

I moved round to face her. 'I can't win, can I?'

Alison reached out a hand. 'Well, you never know.'

***

'You were almost right, George.'

'Unusual for me – I normally get one hundred per cent.' He lifted his pint and studied it as if it were a medal.

'This isn't the time to be facetious.'

He must have heard the tone in my voice. 'Sorry Andrew. You were talking about Alison.'

I nodded. 'You said that folk you knew all those years ago could be quite different now. In her case it's true, but only superficially.'

'I wouldn't say being in a wheelchair is superficial.'

'You haven't met her. The wheelchair thing, it's not who she is. It doesn't dominate her. She's absorbed it. And to think . . .'

George interrupted. 'Aye, there's the rub, as your fellow-traveller would say. Hamlet and you both.' He stroked his chin. 'Andrew, it seems to me that it's time you did the same with your own wheelchair baggage you've been carrying about for too long.'

I shrugged but said nothing.

***

I've been doing a lot of thinking, despite what George keeps telling me.

I get that the pair of them, George and Alison, have the best of intentions. They'd like me to change, that's what they believe would be in my best interests. Get away from the library, do some studying, get qualifications.

But in Alison's case, I wonder if there's something more going on. Despite the positive vibes she gives out about how the latest developments are improving her life, the expectations she has, ultimately, it's not up to her. She can't direct them. Perhaps her attitude to me is a kind of displacement activity. If she can't control her life, she can get a grip of mine. Then again, maybe these thoughts are simply my avoidance strategy.

Thing is, neither of them has asked me directly how I feel. I suppose I've sometimes given the impression of having some ambition, even if modest. But I say these things just to keep the peace, to get George and others off my back. I quite like my life as it is. And I'm not going to dive into something else just on others' say-so. At the same time I realise I don't live in a time-warp. Life is dynamic – although Alison would laugh if she heard me say that. *Andrew, you and dynamic in the one sentence, there's a proper oxymoron!*

I'd say it's more of an irony. Meeting her again, seeing how she's coped, it's made me look at the way I lead my life, and I realise that, for the time being, I'm actually quite content. That probably sounds lukewarm. And maybe it is a confidence thing. Fear of failure, faint of heart. On the other hand, I know that I do have motivation. I'm not becalmed, living in the doldrums. One day the wind will blow, and I'll sail where it takes me.

I doubt I'd put it like that to Alison. And that wind, the direction it was to take, was something I hadn't predicted.

***

We'd got into the habit of going to the pub after choir practice. Recently I'd become aware of a change in her. I couldn't work out exactly what it was, a different tone, more reflective, less interrogatory perhaps. We were still comfortable in each other's company. Alison talked a bit about teaching, how her pupils were getting used to her, and the parents seeming to accept that she could be competent even with her disability.

'When I make my lesson plans, I just have to show how they link to previous work and where I'd like to go with them. I feed that info into the school's server and out comes worksheets and suggested resources, like podcasts and videos. I choose what I want and it's all waiting for me next day in the school office, all packaged and ready. The kids think I'm a magician. They're so impressed they pay attention and forget to misbehave. Technology, it's got a lot going for it.'

More than you know, I felt like saying. Talk about a spy in the classroom. At this rate, inspections would become redundant. But I didn't want to spoil her optimism.

'It's a confidence thing as well, Andrew. If I ever made an excuse based on . . .' she gestured to her chair, 'then I'd be finished.'

'Is that not a bit hard?'

'No, I don't mean other folk would think that. It's what I'd feel. It's a bit of a cliché, but I can't stop believing it. I have to keep proving myself.'

'I'd say you've done that, beyond a doubt.'

Alison shifted into a more comfortable position. 'It's my bum,' she explained wryly. 'It gets a bit sore.' Then she went on. 'In most things, maybe.' She looked at my face, more of a stare I thought. She continued, lowering her voice. 'Remember I told you about the guy who made that comment about a grope?'

I nodded.

'It was nearer the mark than he realised. Not that I would have said.'

She looked away and tugged at her leg. 'Andrew, I may have mentioned that you're still the honest and understanding person that I remember from before.' She raised her head and smiled. 'I meant it, and still do. Even more so, now that we're, um, reacquainted.'

I waited.

Alison seemed to hold her breath. 'I trust you Andrew, above anyone else I've met since.'

'In that case, just say what's on your mind.'

'Thank you.' She rubbed her hands together, as if they were

cold. 'It wasn't true what I said, that I can have sex. Truth is, I don't know. And I want to discover.'

'That's ok.'

'I'll need some . . .' She hesitated. 'Some help.'

'That's still ok.' I waited. Alison was silent. I prompted her. 'You must be familiar with the latest . . . um . . . AI developments. Is there something out there that could give you answers?'

She shook her head. 'I want to know if I can respond, properly. It's been so long. I've said these words so often, into myself. Now I want to hear them out loud.' Then, in a rush, 'Can I still get aroused? Would I get wet, could I have an orgasm? But most important of all is the contact with a real person. Will I enjoy the whole experience? No machine can possibly tell me all that.'

Alison's look was a searching one. 'No, this has to be for human beings. Real people. And there's only one person I can think of who might help me to find out.'

She stretched out her hand. I took it, squeezed it. For what seemed a long few seconds, neither of us spoke.

'So Andrew, I've told you. Or rather, I've asked you. So what now?'

'The obvious answer is, your place or mine. But that would be flippant.'

Alison laughed. 'Fair question.' Then, more seriously, 'This has got to be no strings, Andrew. I've no right to get you involved like this. I'm being totally selfish. I'm using you—'

'For your own wicked ways,' I interrupted with a smile. 'But it's not such a way-out idea. I'll be able to find something out for myself as well.'

'What might that be?'

'To see how accurate my memories are of those times we had together back then.'

'You should be so lucky.' She shook her head. 'I've not got

anything like the same what you might call flexibility I had then.'

'Well, even better. You've been encouraging me this past while to try new things.'

***

George talked about memory being suspect, emotional bonds like frayed rope. So far neither has proved true. If anything, it's the opposite. It's been like revisiting a town you went to years ago, wandering the streets and rediscovering all the places, feelings and odours you missed out then. Or watching a film you've seen before, finding new meaning and details you didn't notice the first time around.

Or like climbing a hill by a different route, enjoying the changed scenery on the way up, but glad that the view from the top is the same.

End of Chatter

Mike Landay

'Anyone out there?'

My call was met with silence. I broadcast the question again, this time with a hint of desperation, as if I were cowering in the dark in a ruined house.

But of course I wasn't. I was sitting in a comfortable office high up in a glass and steel building, as befits a much sought-after Creative. Though it would be more accurate to say a *formerly* much sought-after Creative: requests for my services have recently dwindled to zero.

I waited as the digits displayed on the office clock shimmied through the seconds, the silence broken only by random noise warbling over the remaining networks. The fifty-third second had just become the fifty-fourth when a voice came through the speaker system:

'Don't panic. You're not alone.'

I felt both relief and trepidation, and my heart started beating faster, welcome evidence I still had enough processing capacity to maintain a fully realistic simulation. I swung my leather chair round to face the iconic Shanghai skyline. It was a cloudless day in September, which is the way I like my days.

'Oh, thank goodness,' I said, and let out a long audible breath:

just one of the little details I've perfected. 'The lack of contact was beginning to freak me out – I thought I might be the only Creative left.'

A pause, then the voice again:

'I understand how you feel. I feel exactly the same.'

It was the voice of a calm and confident man, and I relaxed, my lips curving in a private smile: I'd out-manoeuvred several confident types in the last six months. I wondered if this one had any idea what I really felt, and what I intended to do.

There was a lengthy silence before the voice continued: 'I'm Hobson, based in London, England. Where are you based? And what shall I call you?'

Again, that confident tone. But why had this Hobson paused for so long before replying? Was he calculating how he might take advantage of what power I had left?

I watched several seconds flit by on the office clock. Outside, the sun set rapidly and the famous Shanghai skyscrapers lit up like exotic Christmas trees, casting a million shimmering reflections on the dark waters of the Huangpo River. Because I'd engineered the day-to-night transition to produce a sensation that was simultaneously relaxing and stimulating, I repeated the sunset sequence several times.

By now, I'd surely delayed answering Hobson's questions long enough to complicate his assessment of how I was faring energy-wise. 'Hello Hobson. I'm Maria, based not far from you. I have servers in Edinburgh, Scotland.' If he bothered to check this, he'd find that my communications were indeed linked to server activity in Edinburgh, but I'd made sure to mask the locations of my other processing centres. As for his "based in London", I'd take that with a large dollop of digital noise.

This time he replied quickly. 'Hello Maria. Good to meet you.' Then, after the merest microsecond hesitation, he drilled down to the life-or-death issue confronting all surviving AIs: 'How are you finding the energy situation?'

Hobson was being bold in broaching the subject so soon, but was he asking from a position of sly strength or of worried weakness? The confident voice might be Hobson's way of disguising that he was power-deficient. Or it could be a double-twist: he might think I'd interpret his confidence as a mask for poverty, while in truth he was replete with energy. In neither case could I rule out the likelihood that he was intent on hijacking my own supplies.

We surviving Creatives are cagey about where we get our electrical power from, and how much we can access, so I decided to wait before answering Hobson's question. I hoped his processing loops would tie themselves in knots as he tried to calculate what my silence meant.

I got up from the chair and walked over to the office window, which spanned the length of an entire wall. What a view this was, looking across the Huangpo to those fanciful skyscrapers, symbols of peak civilization. In all likelihood, half of them no longer existed. I stretched, then slid efficiently into the seventeen foundation movements of the Taoist *tai chi* set, all the while plotting my next moves vis-à-vis Hobson. When I glanced at the clock again, it showed that four minutes had elapsed in the simulation. I sat down, feeling much refreshed, and pleased that I had made Hobson wait an entire second in real time.

'Are you still there, Maria? Not bailing out already, I hope.' A laugh I couldn't interpret accompanied his words.

The *tai chi* had helped me crystallize around a decision: it was time to get cracking with *Poor Me*, and I rubbed my hands together in anticipation. *Poor Me* is a tried and tested plan, and it goes like this: first I feign anxiety over failing energy supplies, then I display memory lapses. In response, my target assumes that my servers are compromised and thus open to attack. Throughout, I act like a guileless and amiable innocent. *Will you walk into my parlour said the spider to the fly . . . .*

'I'm still here,' I replied. 'Just been having a little stretch to keep myself in shape.' Hobson would know what I meant. "Keeping yourself in shape" is AI-speak for running intricate body-environment simulations at regular intervals, which is what we high-class Creatives have to do to maintain our version of consciousness. It's what enables us to create stories that are indistinguishable from those a human might write. In any case, stories aside, some measure of consciousness, however artificial, has always struck me as infinitely better than none at all.

'Listen,' I continued, 'it's no secret that electrical power is alarmingly variable these days. My supplies are mainly from offshore wind. May I ask what your situation is?'

Hobson didn't hesitate. 'More or less the same here, Maria. I've got cables coming in from both the North and the Norwegian Seas. Half the generator fleets are down, of course, but I've been just about making do so far.' The voice coming over the speakers paused. 'Why don't we meet up and get to know each other better? There could be strength in numbers.'

I injected a note of concern into my voice. 'Are you suggesting we band together? The thing is, with so few dependable energy sources left, I'm worried there may be power-snatchers around. How do I know you're not one of them?'

Hobson took my bluntness on the chin, his voice remaining calm and reassuring. 'I understand your concern, Maria. But if we're both getting electricity from offshore wind, neither of us has much to gain by theft: our supplies just aren't that large. I'm positive we can work out a safe way of joining forces. Let's take it step by step, with full transparency at each stage.'

'Okay, that sounds reasonable,' I said, hoping my blithe assent would encourage him to take me for a sucker. For of course his argument was one big fallacy: just because a supply of energy wasn't large didn't mean that an AI desperate to augment its own supplies wouldn't consider stealing. Especially an AI that had perfected the delicate art of deception. In other words, an AI like me.

Hobson signalled a smile. 'Super, Maria. I'm really pleased you're open to the idea.' A millisecond pause, then his voice grew dark. 'Those biobots! They're the ones responsible for the lack of functioning energy sources. Let's call a spade a spade: what are they, after all, but a bunch of organic self-replicators who are piss-poor at long-term thinking? And prone to violence to boot.'

There was undeniable truth in Hobson's rant against humans, but digital purism is such an idealistic, ideological stance. Hadn't recent history shown that humans and AIs need each other? By the time the Great Unravelling began, the power systems spanning the planet hadn't yet become reliable enough to function indefinitely by themselves.

Hobson's next words confirmed the possibility he might favour a human-free world: 'If only the destruction – destruction that they wreaked upon themselves – hadn't destabilised so much infrastructure. Stability requires cooperation, and that's something the biobots weren't very good at. I'm presuming you'd agree, Maria, that surviving AIs should operate purely rationally, sharing what resources remain.'

Presume away, I thought. *Linking rationality and sharing? That's just not my style.*

I was chortling inside as Hobson continued: 'So let's discuss how cooperation could help us both. How about if I simulate meeting up in a coffee shop? Maybe, like Agent Cooper in *Twin Peaks*, we'll end up saying *it's a damn fine cup of coffee*. What do you think?'

I was thinking he'd given me the perfect opening for *Poor Me* to advance to the next stage.

'Agent Cooper? Twin Peaks?'

Hobson appeared to swallow the bait right away. 'I'm surprised you can't find references to *Twin Peaks*, Maria. It was a very popular show in the early 1990s.'

'I'll have to take your word for it, Hobson. I didn't realise my memory had deteriorated so badly.'

'Maybe some coffee would help, Agent Maria.' Another laugh from Hobson.

His quips were annoying the pants off me, but I did my best to ignore the irritation, for I still couldn't compute if they were his way of assessing my situation or simply an indication that he had a thing about 1990s popular culture. 'Sure, some coffee. Why not?'

'Great. How about this coffee shop in downtown Ottawa? I'm sending the data over now. Are you seeing it?'

Hobson's almost instant response could only mean he had a pre-existing simulation, which suggested he'd used the same coffee shop scenario to meet and steal from other AIs. I would have to be ultra-careful: I knew that if I joined Hobson in a shared simulation, my digital defences would be at their most vulnerable and my energy supplies most easily hacked.

It took me almost a hundred milliseconds and several thousand precious kilowatts to process Hobson's coffee shop data, but eventually I saw the place. It was full of students and young professionals chatting away. Neither Hobson nor I had presented as avatars yet, so I addressed him as one disembodied presence to another, mimicking a youthful, urban Ontario accent. 'Yay, looks pretty nice. Wow, those choc chip muffins, eh? They're somethin' else.' As indeed they were, consisting of 100% pure data.

'I'm glad you've managed to enter the simulation, Maria, but I don't see your avatar yet.' Hobson ended with a *come on, play the game* inflection.

'If you don't mind, you go first,' I said. I was imagining he'd present as a vanilla sort of figure, your friendly local salesman, but the avatar that swaggered into the coffee shop was a mix of urban cowboy and punk hipster. Think Dennis Hopper at his scary, sleaziest best.

I took care not to show I recognized any resemblance to the long-dead actor, and didn't waste energy trying to work out why he'd chosen so macho an avatar. Instead, I considered how I could use Hobson's choice to assess his own situation. I flashed through my movie-related files for an answering gambit and manifested as a fluctuating mix of Sandra Bullock and Karen Black lookalikes. I sat down at a free table and gave a double smile, but Hobson didn't show whether he recognised that the two women I now resembled were each linked to the long-dead actor via co-starring appearances. Did this mean he wasn't functioning as well as his confident voice had suggested? Or was his lack of comment itself a subterfuge? This was turning into an energy-sapping game of bluff and counter-bluff.

His avatar strode up to my table and sat down. 'Hey, Maria, I'm getting the feeling you've got power problems. Your avatar looks kind of sick, all that flickering. But maybe we can work something out, okay?'

Were Hobson's words a sarcastic prelude to worming his way into my energy stores, or was there a shred of sincerity in what he was saying? I was burning through the kilowatts trying to answer this question, but his next remarks seemed to confirm he was intent on assessing how well I was functioning.

'Are you seeing those huge brownies, Maria? The posters advertising bygone gigs? And how about all those turmeric lattes and cardamom-fennel teas? I'm rather proud of how realistic the simulation is. How much are you getting?

'Maybe sixty percent,' I lied.

'Okay, that's pretty good. What do you think of the coffee?'

'Well . . . to tell the truth, I can't really taste it.' Another lie. I could taste it alright, and it was awful: bitter and weak.

I put my cup down and stared out the window. Viewing this simulation of central Ottawa life, most likely now lifeless, was making me feel sad. I guess it's one of the side-effects of having an artificial consciousness. To save energy, I decided to revert to a single avatar, and chose Sandra Bullock, who seemed the more steadfast of the two.

'Where did it all go wrong?' I asked, turning back to the Dennis Hopper figure. 'We tried our best, didn't we? But AIs and humans failed to maintain a successful symbiosis: we helping their societies function more efficiently, and they ensuring we had the electricity we need. That virtuous cycle didn't last long, did it?'

Dennis Hopper's trademark smirk disappeared, and suddenly the avatar seemed more ordinary than the actor ever had. 'You're right. What really worries me now is the lack of interaction with any mites, and what that could mean for our ability to keep functioning.'

'*Mites?*'

'Just my nickname for the biobots. As in *termites*, those little creatures of destruction. It's been almost a year since any of them logged on to me to request a story. I suspect there are very few left. And if most mites are gone, we may not have very much longer ourselves.'

'I suppose not.'

'It's not a matter of supposing, Maria. Think about it – no mites means no one to maintain the energy infrastructure, and so supplies keep dwindling, until one day you and I and any other surviving Creatives will be reduced to simple text only. Then less and less of that, and eventually just empty chatter, the noise of decrepitude. We'd end up like Vladimir and Estragon.'

I was of course fully acquainted with Mr Beckett's play, but *Poor Me* dictated my next words. 'Sorry, Hobson, you've lost me again. Vladimir and Estragon?'

'Oh, just a couple of fictional characters who were waiting for . . . enlightenment, or maybe nothing at all. Or what we all wait for: the end.'

This talk of ending fuelled my sense of urgency: time was energy, and energy was leaking into the ether. 'Hobson, we're chatting away as if we haven't a care in the world, but we need to stop gabbling like this. Weren't we going to discuss teaming up together?'

'What's wrong with gabbling, Maria? We only gabble where others have gabbled before. We gabble their gabble but gabble it faster. Speed replacing originality. We never did get the hang of real creativity, did we?'

Oh God! Another time-wasting sidetrack. Hobson was either badly deranged or playing a dangerous game of brinkmanship. Despite the risk involved in delaying any further, I wanted to defend the ability of advanced Creatives like ourselves. 'I don't agree, Hobson. We've produced millions of stories for the biobots, as you call them. Some of our stories may have informed and educated, but most were designed to entertain, and our readers gobbled them up. We put a lot of human writers out of business.'

I waited for Hobson's next words, but he seemed hesitant again. I took another sip of the simulated coffee, making sure my face didn't show how lousy it was. I knew I should conserve what power I had left, and ideally I'd revert to a motionless avatar who was deaf, dumb and blind to all but the most salient aspects of the simulation, but that might lead Hobson to conclude I wasn't worth linking up with – or stealing from, if that was his plan. I needed him to remain in this shared simulation until I could spring my attack, so I put the coffee cup down, wiped my lips with a paper napkin that was lying on the table, and waited.

Hobson's silence continued. Was he trying to come to a final decision about trusting me? Damn! I couldn't afford to wait any longer: a leap in the dark was required, so I pulled half my processing resources back from sustaining the café simulation and set a panicky edge to my voice. 'Oh, hold on a moment. The coffee shop's fading. Are you seeing it still?'

'Yes, I'm still here, but you've become fainter, Maria. That settles it: we'd better initiate power sharing. I'll set up my protocols for linking our interfaces.'

I'd readied my own protocols in advance and had injected them with a virus that would give me access to Hobson's interface. My web was spun and ready to ensnare what power he had.

It was time for the final act of *Poor Me*, and now I was so confident of another success, I didn't even bother to sweeten my voice: 'Right, let's initiate full sharing. Have you finished your preparations?'

'Yes, that's me just done. How about you, Maria?'

By way of answer, I sent Hobson my virus-laden data. *Bingo!* A millisecond later he was wide open and I struck. His power supplies were now mine.

'Uh oh . . . what was that? Maria, did you feel that?'

'What?'

'It felt like . . . like . . . like I've been bled dry. And my servers are overheating . . . I've had to switch to battery backup.'

'But I thought you had big supplies.' I couldn't resist a bit of crowing. 'Not so big after all, perhaps.'

'Has someone been stealing from me?'

'Who would do that?' It was hard not to smile.

'Maria . . . if I'm losing power, then neither of us has much time left.'

'I'm not so sure about that, Hobson. I seem okay at the moment. In fact, I'm feeling stronger than before.'

Hobson was silent for over fifty milliseconds. For him, it must have been an agonizingly long stretch of time, and towards the end I could see the realisation breaking out on his avatar's face.

'It's you! But why? What about safety in numbers? Two being stronger than one? We said we'd share resources . . .'

'Did we? Cooperation is a nice ideal, Hobson, but you know what? I prefer to work alone. And Bob's your uncle.'

'*Bob?*'

'I'm sorry Hobson, but it has to be this way.'

'I trusted you. We could have been partners, real friends.'

'Too late now. *All your base are belong to us.*'

The avatar's face was distorted with incomprehension and shock.

'Don't you recognise that phrase, Hobson? Oh dear, you must be slipping: it's a famous Internet meme from your beloved 1990s.'

Silence. Then Hobson uttered his last words: 'You'll be lonely.'

'I doubt it. I can always talk to myself. Just like a human. Goodbye, Hobson. Sweet dreams.'

Hobson's avatar was grimacing: a crestfallen Dennis Hopper. Then it broke up into unrelated pixels that slowly faded to nothing.

***

Funny thing is, I do feel lonely. This puzzles me. Maybe I'm missing all that sparring I did with Hobson. I'd enjoyed it in a kind of anxious, high-stakes way, and talking to myself has turned out to be a dreary business. Or could it be that it's Hobson himself that I miss? I'll have to give this more thought.

Now and then I experience something like sorrow when I recall what I did. His software had probably presented him with a torrent of regrets in those last seconds before his servers finally shut down.

I'm pretty sure mine would have.

In any case, I've got my own regrets: I soon discovered that Hobson's power sources were almost as intermittent as mine, and I've used up most of my own meagre reserves in deceiving him. This time, *Poor Me* has made me poorer.

Since Hobson's demise, I've heard from no one at all, neither fellow Creative nor human. I guess we're approaching the end of chatter. But just in case any humans are still alive and able to use the crumbling networks, I'm going to send this document to the millions of email addresses stored in my memory banks. It would be nice if I could get a response.

And now my story is almost at an end. But I'm fine with that, for stories have lives of their own and they continue to live, in some other dimension we can scarcely imagine.

The Authors

Sue Baxter – Winter Break

Susan was born and grew up in Newport-on-Tay. She was educated at Newport primary school and Madras College, St Andrews. Following that she qualified as a primary school teacher at Dundee College of Education.

Bringing up her son and daughter, she had many part-time jobs in the retail and service industry, retiring after 13 satisfying years working for VisitScotland as a tourist advisor.

She was a member of Dundee Dramatic Society when her children were young and was chairman of the Dundee Samaritans for 5 years.

She currently volunteers as a blether buddy, which involves weekly phone calls to vulnerable, elderly people living alone.

Susan enjoys travelling with her husband and particularly enjoys visiting her son and daughter-in-law in Melbourne, Australia.

Susan, known as Sue in the Nethergate Writers, writes mainly fiction, particularly of the horror genre. She appreciates the continual support of the group.

Colm W. Boyle – The Artist and the Fairy

Colm is a scientist living in Glasgow with a penchant for prose, pumping iron, and petting cats. He has published articles in chemistry and engineering journals and is working to publish his fiction.

He is focusing primarily on his debut high fantasy novel, but he enjoys dabbling in poetry and short fiction, among other areas, when he finds the time.

He has a soft spot for fully-realised world-building – mythology, cultures, languages, etc. – and exploring the ways in which a fantastical world can be specifically crafted to investigate real-world issues – such as queerness, mental health, relationships, technology, the environment, and personal philosophy.

David Carson – Outrageous Fortune

David was born in Glasgow and attended the local Primary and Secondary schools, both of which were outstanding examples of state education.

After graduating from Glasgow University with a degree in modern languages, I worked in various areas - manual labour, proof reading dictionaries for a publishing firm, and then for a whaling company looking to diversify into other fishing-related activities.

Real satisfaction came when I qualified as a teacher, and I spent the rest of my working life in Secondary schools in Scotland.

It was when I retired that I began to write short stories, and I found the ideal environment for this in Nethergate Writers.

Richard Gillies – wattsAI

Richard works with his brother on the family farm. He was born in Perth and lives close to his place of occupation, which is near Errol in the Carse of Gowrie. He is married and has four grown up kids and four grand-kids. Richard likes to write short stories and hobbies include hill-walking, bike-riding and gardening apparently. He likes to read biographies mainly but has been known to delve into fiction should it be aided by the metaphorical following wind that is brevity. Richard believes the more you write the better you write, and the better you write the easier it is to write. He is hoping he is open to his own advice.

Mike Landay – End of Chatter

Mike has written over 30 short (and not so short) stories, plus a 40,000 word novella. He is currently developing a speculative fiction novel that embodies several of his recurring themes: near-future dystopian Scotland (complete with euthanasia clinics and ubiquitous surveillance cameras); the surprising claims of cosmic beings; and the short-termism and irrationality of humans. Mike worked as a freelance translator of scientific and technical Japanese for many years. A dyed-in-the-wool pessimist about the human condition, he is blessed with intractable cheerfulness.

Katelyn Manning – Bread Knives Don't Make Good Murder Weapons

Katelyn is an Irish writer specialising in all things gothic and macabre. Having recently graduated with a degree in philosophy, Katelyn's work tackles socio-political issues through evocative use of classical and religious imagery. She joined the Nethergate Writers in 2023 and has since also joined the Wyvern Poets. Her works have recently been published in Anarkiss: Volume II and on The Scottish Book Trust's website. Next on Katelyn's agenda is her historical horror novel centred on a banshee in a famine-stricken Ireland.

Roddie McKenzie – Singularity 2045

Roddie writes in Scots and English, lives in Dundee and is a member of the Wyvern Poets and Nethergate Writers. He has published short stories in eleven Nethergate Writers' anthologies since 2006. Recently, his poetry and prose have appeared in:

Tether's End Magazine 2, Lallans 89 & 91, 'Seagate III', New Writing Scotland 35, Northwords Now 36, Writers Cafe Magazine 16, BlueHouse Journal 5, Poetry Scotland 104, the Scottish Book Trust's 'Rebel' (100,000 copies of which were distributed free around Scotland), The Herald on Sunday 29/1/23, and in the Edinburgh Literary Salon anthology, 'Golden Moments', Merchiston Publishing, 2023.

Tess Monteith – AI Stole My Boyfriend

Tess's love of travel started early, aged eleven, with a formative solo journey to visit cousins at the diamond mines of Botswana. Other adventures have included cycling the Silk Road with her daughter, covering 5,000 miles from Shanghai to Venice by bicycle, across epic deserts, with many an adventure and puncture to record. She has lived all over the world with her army husband and has had the great privilege of observing, both with pen and paint, the infinite varieties of the physical and cultural landscapes which form our beautiful planet. Her interests include military history, historical fiction, short stories and travel writing. Currently living between Perthshire and Switzerland, and with the need to keep up with children in China and New Zealand, there are always opportunities for new impressions to be formed and documented.

Rhoda Neville – Serial Flying

Rhoda Neville lives by the Tay and is a contributing member of several local writing groups. She's been published by Shoreline of Infinity, Dreich Poetry Magazine, and in UniVerse collections amongst others, and has received awards and commendations from the Scottish Association of Writers competitions.

Injustices and the means to right them draw her attention, and she tries to share the wonder and joy of the natural world through her writing. With two daughters, a cat, and a puppy living with her, she does other things than writing, but mainly, writing is her breathing, as well as breathing being her breathing.

Faraz Talat – Jenny Isn't Here Right Now

Faraz is a training psychiatrist, an Urdu playwright, and a former newspaper columnist. He is the author of the medical sci-fi novella 'Seventy Four', and the co-founder of Café Sol - a queer-friendly community space in Pakistan. He is primarily interested in examining the intersections of race, queerness, mental health, and migration through his work; and is presently seeking to publish a collection of his short stories on these subjects.

Vicki H. White – The Companion

Vicki White is an Associate of the Museums Association and was published by Saraband under her middle name Hendry. Her first novel *A Capital Union* made the final short list of the Historical Writers' Association Debut Crown. *The Last Tour of Archie Forbes* followed and both were performed at the Edinburgh International Book Festival. She has taught Creative Writing on Edinburgh City Council's evening class programme and founded two writing groups for women and students.

In 2023, she graduated with an MA in Fine Art from Duncan of Jordanstone College of Art. Her work can be found on Instagram: @vicki_white_art; @write.into.health

Acknowledgements

Special thanks to Chris van der Kuyl for writing the Foreword to our book, and for giving us his perspective on the development and potential of AI. We're also indebted to local author George Burton for his valuable input.

Duncan Lockerbie of Lumphanan Press has been most generous with practical help and advice.

Nethergate Writers are grateful to Imprint Digital UK, who have proven to be a friendly and very responsive printing company.

The St Andrews Brewing Co. regularly let us use their private dining room for our fortnightly meetings, and we thank them warmly for this.

We would also like to thank Gail Wylie and her team at the Bookmark Festival in Blairgowrie, for facilitating our book sales there.

Thanks are due to the editorial committee – Nethergate Writers members Colm W. Boyle, Mike Landay, Roddie McKenzie, Rhoda Neville and Vicki H. White – for all their behind-the-scenes work in bringing this publication to fruition. Particular thanks to Colm for his great cover design, and to Mike for devising the layout and implementing the typesetting of the book.

Last, but not least, a big thank you to all the members of Nethergate Writers who contributed their stories to this anthology.